Revolt

Vernon Coleman

©Vernon Coleman 2010. The right of Vernon Coleman to be identified as the author of this work has been asserted in accordance with the Copyright, Designs and Patents Act 1988. This book was first published under the pen name Robina Hood.

Vernon Coleman is the bestselling author of over 100 books – many of which are now available on Amazon as Kindle books. For a full list of books available please see Vernon Coleman's author page on Amazon or search for 'Vernon Coleman Kindle'. Vernon Coleman's books have sold over two million hardback and paperback copies in the UK and been translated into 25 languages.

All characters, organisations and businesses in this book are fictitious, and any resemblance to real persons (living or dead), organisations or businesses is purely coincidental.

A political satire.

Based on a true story
that hasn't happened yet.

Chapter 1

Tom opened the cupboard beside the oven and rummaged around. He tried to do so quietly, but it is difficult to move pots and pans without making a noise.

'What are you doing love?' his aunt asked.

'I'm looking for something heavy,' whispered Tom, pulling an aluminium saucepan out of the cupboard. It is, he thought, dangerous to be right when the Government is wrong. But maybe, he added to himself, as a corollary, it can also be dangerous to work for the Government when the Government is wrong.

'What do you want something heavy for?' his aunt asked. She had lowered her voice to match her nephew's.

'I want to kill someone with it,' whispered Tom. 'I'm going to hit him on the head.' He half heard himself and could hardly believe what he half heard himself say. Though he had always stood up for himself, his beliefs and those he cared for he had always avoided violence. He had played rugby as though the aim of the game was to avoid contact with the ball. At school he had only ever been involved in one fight. An older boy had taunted him with lewd remarks about his mother, younger and considerably more attractive than the mothers of any of his contemporaries. Tom had punched the boy on the nose, leapt upon him and pummelled him until he'd been dragged off. It was his only ever fight. After that the other boys treated him with quiet respect. 'It's got to be heavy,' he repeated, half to himself

'Ah,' said his aunt with a nod of comprehension. 'Then that pan is too light. You need something heavier. The frying pan is iron and much heavier. Try that.' She spoke with as much emotion as if she were suggesting the correct pan for frying eggs.

Tom put the saucepan back and picked up the frying pan which was on the stove. He weighed it in his hand. It seemed well-made and solid. The handle felt good. It fitted his hand nicely. He looked at his aunt, for whom he felt affection and a great sense of responsibility, and then thought about Dorothy, whom he loved dearly, and realised that he really had no other option. He took a deep breath and went back into the hall. His love for Dorothy, and the companionship that had grown out of that love, was all that he had; it was all he had to live for; all that held him together. He would do anything for Dorothy.

'He's dead,' said the sprout, waiting in the hallway. 'You're too damned late. You killed him.' He looked at the frying pan in Tom's hand. 'What the hell is that..?' He stared at the frying pan with disbelief. The sprouts' arrogance made them stupid and careless and more vulnerable than they could think possible.

And that was as far as he got before Tom hit him on the head with the edge of a frying pan.

The sprout fell immediately. To Tom's quiet surprise there was almost no blood.

Tom stood still for a moment. Then he bent down, put his fingers against the sprout's neck and felt for a pulse. The sprout's heart was still beating. Tom raised the frying pan and brought it down even harder. This time some blood seeped from a small, broken vein. The frying pan slipped out of Tom's reach and bounced and slithered down the hallway towards the door to the kitchen. Tom checked again. The man still had a pulse.

'Who's that?'

Horrified, Tom turned. Everything seemed to be happening in slow motion but he was concentrating so hard on what he was doing that he didn't even recognise his aunt's voice. And it was his aunt who was standing in the kitchen doorway.

'A sprout,' answered Tom.
'What on earth is he doing?'
'I hit him.'
'Why did you do that, dear?'
'I wanted to kill him.'
'He's not dead.'
'No. I know that, auntie.'
'So, hit him again!'
'I can't get to the frying pan.'
'Use his shoe.'

Tom tore the man's shoe from his foot and banged him on the head with it. The shoe simply bounced off the man's head.

'It's got a rubber sole. I don't think hitting him with it is doing him any good but it's not going to kill him.' Tom felt hot and sticky. He had pains everywhere; the ones in his chest and down his arms were the most worrying. He wiped sweat from his forehead with his sleeve.

'It's not supposed to be doing him any good. You're trying to kill him. What's that awful smell?'

'It's corning from his shoes.'

'His shoes?'

'He must have stepped in something on the way here.'

Tom's aunt looked at the sole of the shoe her son was holding, wrinkled her nose and turned away her head. 'Ugh! How disgusting. He's a sprout?'

'Yes.'

'I thought he was,' she said, with a nod. 'He's got very smelly shoes.'

Just then the first sprout stirred and groaned. Tom jumped.

'He's not dead either!' said Tom's aunt. 'You'll have to hit them both again.'

'We could electrocute them,' said Tom. 'I've seen them do it in films. We put them into a bath full of water and then throw in an electrical appliance of some kind.'

His aunt looked at him.

'An electric fire. A toaster. Something like that.'

'The only electric fire we have is fixed into the wall in my bedroom and it doesn't work.' She waved a hand towards the frying pan. 'Give that thing to me.'

Tom hesitated.

'Give it to me.' She pointed. 'The pan thing.'

Tom stood up, fetched the frying pan and turned back to hand it to his aunt. But she'd disappeared. He went back into the kitchen. She wasn't there. He went back into the hallway and saw her coming out of the living room. She was wearing a golf glove on her left hand. She had never played golf in her life, though Tom's father had been a keen golfer. Tom didn't know they still had one of his golf gloves.

'Give me the pan,' she said.

Tom handed her the frying pan and watched in astonishment as she swung it above her head and brought it down first onto the head of one sprout and then onto the head of the other.

'We can't have bodies at the bottom of the stairs,' complained his aunt, peering at the sprouts to see what damage she had done. 'We will have to move them. I can't be clambering over bodies at my age every time I want to go to the bathroom. I might trip up.'

'I'm sorry.'

'How many are there?'

'How many what?'

'Bodies.'

'Just the two.'

'Oh. I wondered if there might be more. Still, when you're trying to get around, one is plenty but two are far too many.'

'They're sprouts, auntie. I killed them.'

'I wondered who they were. I didn't recognise them. Are they anyone I know?'

'I don't think so, auntie.'

'Your grandfather killed Germans in the war. They gave him medals for it.' Tom's aunt had been diagnosed as suffering from mild dementia, though Tom was often painfully aware that the adjective 'mild' is invariably applied subjectively.

'I know.'

'He had a German helmet. Kept it at the back of the wardrobe. They didn't give him that. He took it. Black with a big spike on the top.'

Tom didn't want his aunt to get too involved with memories of her father. He enjoyed talking to her about the past but this didn't seem to be a suitable moment.

'They came to check on our labels.'

'He kept it in the wardrobe because my mum was worried that my brother or I might hurt ourselves on it.'

'What?'

'The helmet.'

'These two were label inspectors,' said Tom, trying to turn his aunt's attention back to the present.

'Well, don't worry about it. I expect they've got plenty more of these people.'

'I've killed them!'

'Were they German?'

'No. They were Romanian.'

'Oh, that's all right then. As long as they were foreign. Do you think they'll give you a nice medal? Who do we have to tell for you to get a medal?'

'They won't give me a medal. But they might have me killed.'

'No medals? Your granddad got medals for killing foreigners.

Have they changed the rules? Why on earth would they kill you? Is killing Romanians a bad thing to do? It's a pity they weren't German.'

Tom paused for a moment. 'They might think it's a bad thing.'

'And they will want to punish you for it?'

'They will if they find out.'

'Oh dear. Well, that's outrageous. What is the world coming to? No one ever threatened to lock up your granddad. He was given his medals by a General. How dead are they?'

'I don't think there are varieties of dead, aunt. There aren't stages as there are with drunkenness or wickedness. You're pretty much either dead or you're not.' Tom loved his aunt but he was beginning to realise that she was perhaps not the best person to have at his side at what he thought he could fairly describe as something of a crisis.

'And they're definitely dead?'

'Yes.'

'Are you sure? Is this one totally dead?' She poked the body of the second sprout with the toe of her pink fluffy slipper.

'Completely, utterly, totally dead.'

'Does he know?' She poked him again, bent down and peered at him very carefully.

'The dead man?'

'Of course, dear. Who else are we talking about?' Tom sighed. 'Yes, aunt, the dead man knows.'

'Hmm. Well, I wouldn't say he is dead. If you want him to be dead you're going to have to hit him on the head again with something pretty solid.'

It was at that moment that the dead body, irritated by all the nudging, sat up, rubbed his head and looked around. As might be expected he looked confused and rather bewildered by his circumstances.

Without hesitation Tom's aunt raised the frying pan above her head and brought it down as though it were a golf club and she was playing a drive with one hand. It hit the side of the sprout's head with a fearsome crack.

'There you are,' said Tom's aunt. 'That's the way to do it.' She smiled at him.

'Thanks,' said Tom, quietly.

'That made me feel better,' she said. 'I've been very pissed off for much longer than you have.'

Chapter 2

None of this would have happened if Tom hadn't been upstairs painting a cupboard.

Tom Cobleigh didn't like unexpected visitors and had long ago disconnected the front doorbell, unfastening one of the wires so that when callers pressed the button attached to the door jamb nothing happened inside the house.

He had kept the bell push, rather than simply removing it and throwing it away, in the hope that callers would assume that, since they had pressed the bell push, then a bell must have rung somewhere in the house and, would, therefore, leave satisfied that they had made their presence felt but that the house had been unoccupied at the time of their visit.

'Most people respond to bells,' explained Tom who had read more than most people about Pavlov and his dogs. 'Telephone bells, doorbells, it doesn't matter what sort of bell it is, most people respond when they hear them. And so those same people assume that other people behave the same way. They believe that if a bell is rung, and heard, it will be dignified with a response. And that conversely, if a bell is rung and there is no response then there must be no one there to hear it ring.'

His friends, few in number though they were, constantly argued with him about this, though there were, they knew, many other things that were far more worthy of argument than the importance, or otherwise, of answering doorbells.

'The point of having a bell,' explained one, 'is so that you can tell when there is someone at the door, respond to their presence and see what they want.'

'That's exactly the point,' agreed Tom. 'It's always about what they want. When do people ever come to the front door with good news? No one ever rings my doorbell to bring me something I want. They always want something from me. They want to tell me I haven't paid my television licence or they want to sell me something. They want to ask me for a donation or to ask me to take out a subscription to something. They want to offer to paint my house or they want their ball back. They want me to do something that will help them.'

'But if you don't open the door you can't let anyone in!'

'Precisely! I never let anyone in unless I want to see them, know they are coming and, most importantly of all, know why they are coming. And if I want to see them and know they are coming, I undo the bolt on the back gate and they come in that way.'

Tom's aunt, who was tiptoeing, unsteadily but with quiet determination, into the world of senility, and who had journeyed some distance into the land where truth and reality have become slightly hazy memories, but fantasy and paranoia have not yet completely replaced them, didn't understand any of this. When she heard a telephone ring she answered it. And when she heard a doorbell ring, she answered it. If she'd heard a dinner gong sound, and had known what it signified, she would have probably responded to that too. Pavlov would have approved of her. He would have been proud of her. She was a woman after his own heart; a woman with sensible reflexes. And so she also opened the front door when people knocked on it.

Before she came to live with Tom she had, for a week, been in a hospital after collapsing at home. She'd had a stroke and had been found in her hallway, semi-conscious and almost moribund. A neighbour had called an ambulance and, in the mistaken belief that they were dealing with a sprout (why would anyone call an ambulance for someone who wasn't a sprout?), the ambulance men had delivered her to the local hospital.

A word of explanation is in order.

The people of Europe had been divided into two groups: those fortunate individuals who worked for what had been the European Union but was now known as the États-Unis de Communauté Européenne (referred to as EUDCE), and its various subsidiary authorities, commissions and bodies (individuals known formally as officers and informally as sprouts because they were all controlled from EUDCE's permanent headquarters in Brussels) and those far less fortunate folk who didn't (known officially as habitants and equally unofficially as civilians or, more commonly, as suspects because that's how they were regarded).

A week later, when he eventually found out where she'd been taken (a neighbour of his aunt's had told a friend who'd told someone who knew Tom) Tom had visited her there and had found her starving, lying between filthy sheets, in a filthy bed on a filthy ward.

A falling out among relatives meant that he hadn't seen much of his aunt when he'd been small, and had hardly recognised her when he'd met her again. He was sad about that. She'd always sent him birthday and Christmas presents when he'd been a boy and they'd been trains and cars too, instead of the socks and handkerchiefs favoured by most of his other female relatives.

She'd had an adventurous life. Eccentric, big, blonde and boisterous she'd worked as a magician's assistant until she'd grown too big (in all directions) to fit into the box. Unable to earn a living being sawn in half, she'd moved gracefully and naturally into jobs behind a series of bars. She'd been a born barmaid.

'Excuse me, but my aunt looks dehydrated,' said Tom to one of the nurses when he visited the hospital. 'And she's lost a lot of weight. Do you know if there is a reason for that?'

'She won't drink and she won't feed herself,' snapped the nurse.

'She had a stroke,' Tom pointed out.

'She's over that now.'

'But she's confused,' said Tom. 'Shouldn't someone feed her?'

'This isn't a restaurant,' snapped the nurse.

'I wouldn't expect her to be fed in a restaurant,' said Tom. 'But isn't this supposed to be a hospital?'

'We don't feed patients,' said the nurse, lifting her jaw and skewering him with a glare she probably used to strip paint. 'We're professionals. We have other, more important things to do.'

'But if she carries on at this rate she'll starve to death,' Tom pointed out.

The nurse shrugged. 'She's well over 80,' she said. 'We don't have to do anything with the over 60's. Anyway, she'll be going home tomorrow.' She sniffed. 'And she shouldn't have been admitted. She's not entitled.' Tom's aunt's big problem was that she was suspect not a sprout. Suspects weren't entitled to any sort of medical care or residential support.

And old suspects were definitely on the not-wanted list. The sprouts in Brussels had announced plans to make it a legal requirement for suspects over the age of 60 to join a proposed involuntary euthanasia programme. They were going to call it the Life Release Programme and those who enrolled would be paid a small fee in recognition of their commitment. The fee would be just enough to pay for a modest funeral. The scheme was considered an integral part of the two-tone civilisation created by the hierarchy in Brussels. Suspects who reached the age of 59 would be invited to attend classes and take a degree course to prepare them for the end. They would be given a copy of a glossy magazine called Dying, the production of which would, it was hoped, be subsidised with advertisements from appropriate and enterprising businesses. They would also receive a set of six coasters celebrating modem post-Lisbon Treaty European history and the promise that their names would appear on a Roll of Honour on a EUDCE sponsored website. Like all degree courses the whole merry venture would end not with an orthodox examination (such interventions had for years been forbidden as both dangerously elitist and woefully discriminatory) but with a ceremony where all candidates who had attended the requisite number of classes would be given the details of the website upon which their graduation diploma could be found.

'Going home!' said Tom, astonished. 'She can't possibly look after herself'

'That's not our problem,' the nurse said coldly. 'Your aunt's health is of no concern to us. She's a suspect and she's way over the age limit. That's two strikes. Two strikes and you're definitely out. She's not entitled to hospital care.' Sprouts didn't lie much, not to suspects. There was no buttering up. Sticking to the plain, unvarnished truth wasn't something sprouts did because they were honest, or didn't have anything to hide, but because they didn't have to worry about suspects knowing things. The truth was that sprouts didn't worry about anything because only sprouts could punish sprouts and sprouts never punished other sprouts for doing bad things to suspects. Sprouts, even low-grade sprouts, were always assumed to be in the right. Suspects were always in the wrong. Simple. The sprouts were special. And by any measure they were treated as special. They had guaranteed pensions, special health care facilities, special traffic lanes (which weren't entirely necessary since they were the only people who could afford motor cars or the petrol to put into their tanks), special schools and special everything. The sprouts were a different group. They really had become 'them'.

Sprouts inherited their jobs, or came by them through family contacts, and they held them for life, living well and comfortably.

Although it didn't appear in any of the treaties or the constitution, it was the first law of the new United States of Europe and it at least made life simple. Everyone knew where they stood, even if they weren't standing quite where they wanted to stand.

Chapter 3

Tom took his aunt home. Naturally, they made him sign a form taking responsibility for her health and welfare. The sprouts had all the authority but none of the responsibility. He and his wife nursed her back to health; sharing with her the little food they had for themselves.

'Old age is a shipwreck,' said his aunt one day. And Tom could see what she meant. Every moment was a crisis. She was constantly fighting to survive amidst the storms, sharks and cannibals of aching joints, fluttering heart and clogged-up piping. 'If you think life is exhausting when you're young, you just wait until you're old,' his aunt warned him.

But she didn't want to die. 'Not ready yet,' she said firmly. She spent her days watching the Telescreen and looking at old photographs. She often got the two mixed up; confusing the activities of the people she'd seen on the Telescreen and the folk with whom she'd spent the earlier decades of her long life.

Only one channel was available on the Telescreen. All programmes were made, approved and broadcast by the Brussels Broadcasting Corporation, known as the BBC. The BBC was EUDCE's official broadcaster. Most programmes were made in Turkish but all programmes were available in a choice of over thirty languages. All the viewer had to do was set the default on their Telescreen to broadcast in their chosen language.

To get back to the doorbell that didn't ring.

'There's someone here,' shouted Tom's aunt. 'Two someones. They say they're men from...' she struggled to remember what she'd been told and then extemporised. 'Somewhere,' she said, throwing the word away as though it didn't really matter where they came from.

'Did you send them away?'

'No, dear. They sort of pushed their way in when I answered the door.' she said. 'They knocked a lot,' she added, in explanation. 'They just kept knocking.'

'Oh. Where are they?'

'They're in the living room reading the cushions.'

Tom was in the bathroom painting a small cupboard he'd found in a jumble sale. He'd bought it with a trowel one of the allotment holders had given him as a tip for helping clear away some weeds. He balanced his paintbrush on top of the pot of paint, wiped his hands down the sides of his faded green corduroy trousers, and sighed. For a simple exhalation there was a lot of emotion in it. Tom was so full of weariness that it spilt out of him at the slightest provocation.

If the visitors were reading the cushions they would be Soft Artefact Label Inspectors. In the wonderful new world of EUDCE every sprout had a grand tide. Lorry drivers had become Supply Chain Solution Executives. Officer clerks had become Logistical Problem Resolution Officers. And scrapyard employees were known as Conclusion of Active Life Vehicle Disassemblement Centre. If there was doubt the sprout would simply be described as a European Agent of Constitutional Enrichment.

A Label Inspector was only a Grade Three sprout but he was still a sprout; an inspector certified by the authorities and endowed with the full power of arrest and deportation. There were always two of them, of course. Like policemen, bailiffs, small children and girls at dances, sprouts invariably travelled in pairs.

Chapter 4

Tom was 61, tall and slim. This was not particularly through choice or healthy eating but more a consequence of the fact that he never had enough to eat. He had lost much of his hair, had large bags under his eyes and, because of the fluoride they'd put in the drinking water, his teeth were grey.

He wore what he nearly always wore, since they were pretty much the only clothes he owned, a pair of green corduroy trousers that were worn and rather shiny and a sports jacket with leather elbow patches.

He was a sensitive, gentle man who was stronger than he looked and stronger than most people who met him imagined him to be. He was that not uncommon variety of Englishman: a traditionalist who respected history but was not afraid to contemplate new ideas, though he embraced only the ones worth embracing; a man who believed in old-fashioned values without being constrained by bigotry. He was in some ways a very ordinary man but at the same time a most unusual man; a radical who hated change but, at the same time, a man who believed in the widely derided standards of Old England. He was that rare creature: a traditionalist who was never afraid to stand up for what he believed; never afraid to rebel. He was a man who put freedom above all else; he was that combination of cavalier and roundhead that only ever occurs in England.

He was old enough to remember the distant days when ordinary folk were treated with respect by policemen and airport security guards. He could remember when rubbish was collected as a regular routine, by workers not too proud to be known as dustmen, and when civil servants were civil rather than patronising, obliging rather than obstructive. He could even remember when the police responded to emergency calls without asking questions about the ethnicity of both victim and perpetrator. He could remember when muggers and thieves kept to the shadows. (These days the streets were considered so dangerous that one television pundit, sponsored by a failing chain of hamburger restaurants, had suggested that parents should deliberately allow their children to become fat, on the grounds that children who were well-padded with fatty deposits would be less vulnerable to knife attacks.)

Like most male adult suspects Tom wore a beard. The shortage of both water and heat made shaving impractical. Tom, like most of the people he knew, fetched his allocated daily water supply from a standpipe which was turned on for just an hour a day. Hot water, like central heating, was an almost forgotten luxury.

In different times he had worked as a publishing editor. One of his last authors, a reality television star famous mainly for her mammoth, if artificial, bosom had been made a Dame and awarded a Nobel Prize for exceptional services to literature as a result of a series of twelve ghost written autobiographies, all published before her 30th birthday. But the rise of the Internet, the success of what had at the time been known as Google in putting books free onto the Internet and the widespread availability of e-books and authorised free blogs meant that people had stopped buying books. Why bother? Books were too long for most people anyway. Just words, words and more words. No one had read much more than a twitter for years.

As a result Tom, along with printers, bookstores and authors had become just about as employable as a Nazi memorabilia salesman.

He hated the Internet.

Not particularly because it had cost him his job. It had done far more than that. It had destroyed respect for learning, and had destroyed the integrity and honesty of earning. The reliance of web providers on advertising meant that education and scholarship had been taken over by commercial interests. He'd been appalled when a famous breakfast cereal manufacturer had started giving away GCSE certificates with its individually packed products.

'What have you got?' a child would ask, removing a small scroll from the bottom of the packet.

'Arabic,' his brother or sister might reply, doing the same thing. 'That's nine I've got.'

The enthusiasm for free this, free that and free everything else had done what the philistines had never been able to do.

And in the end the governments had taken over the Internet and had learned to control what appeared; to manipulate the content and to suppress the dangerously questioning. It had, for those who had taken the power to themselves, been so very easy.

In the dark and privacy of the night, Tom still dreamt of days when authors and publishers produced daring, iconoclastic books which questioned and undermined the establishment. He had long ago learned that the pen is only mightier than the sword (or the taser) when the person you are facing doesn't actually hold a sword (or a taser) in his hand. He had learned that the pen in the hand of the advertisement buyer writing a cheque is more powerful than the pen in the hand of any independent writer.

Moreover, he no longer believed that most people wanted to know the truth. 'There's what people want to believe,' he had once said, 'there's what people want to hear. And then there is the truth.'

He knew that everyone's future is built upon the relics of their past and that his future was built, for better or worse, on the relic of his past as a publisher. So, it was not much of a future. The only books still being published were the ones produced by what once had been known as the European Union and was now the United States of Europe. All hail, blessed and mighty United States of Europe.

Just that morning an errand boy (a former architect whose practice had been put out of business by legislation endorsing a consortium of EUDCE funded Latvians as priority architects for the region) had delivered a hardback 400-page coffee-table book, printed on glossy paper. The book's title was WRAP (the Waste and Resources Action Programme) and it explained how to avoid waste. It contained a list of 73 separate recycling depots where householders could obtain food stamp credits by delivering such assorted items as used yoghurt cartons, empty beer cans and belt buckles. People who knew and understood the rules, and were prepared to play by them, were rewarded with great riches. Those who didn't know, didn't understand or didn't want to live by the rules were not.

The EUDCE bureaucrats, who had for years neither represented nor respected the people or their views but who had, like all good salesmen, manipulated their own promises to fit what they believed was expected, consistently created rules which harried and punished the hard working and the prudent and which favoured scroungers and thieves.

By the early part of the 21st century, burglars stood a better chance of getting away with their crimes than entrepreneurs had of succeeding with new businesses. (Officially, crime levels had been falling ever since EUDCE had been created and had been at historically low levels for 29 months in succession. Officially.) The man who worked hard to start a business, labouring long into the night and giving his health to create something lasting and worthwhile, was more likely to go bankrupt and end up in prison for debt than the burglar was to go to prison for stealing.

Wearied by a world that was changing in ways he didn't much like, Tom believed that anyone still brave enough to be an optimist was simply someone who didn't know enough.

Through the last quarter of the 20th century and the first years of the 21st century politicians and bureaucrats became increasingly accustomed to making promises they never intended to keep and which, moreover, no one expected them to keep. Members of the electorate, the taxpayers, were regarded as of little or no real consequence, as long as their voting habits could be manipulated satisfactorily. The political class cynically exploited the trusting and the hopeful. Corruption became normal and was so widely accepted that those who were exposed often expressed outrage that they had been criticised for what they regarded as their rights. When politicians and policemen complained about bribery and corruption it was only to moan that they weren't getting enough of it. Most areas of life, business, sport and entertainment, had been tainted by corruption, but politicians and bureaucrats had become consumed by it and none more consumed than those involved in the United States of Europe. Occasionally, there were outbursts of synthetic honesty. For a while, one or two people in public positions vowed to honour promises (unless or until it became necessary or even convenient to do otherwise) but soon even they fell by the wayside. EUDCE bureaucrats (like the politicians who had signed away England's past, present and future, and who had ironically put themselves out of business, were uniformly ambitious, ruthless, utterly lacking in responsibility or any sense of respect or decency; they were driven by pure arrogance and self-regard.

In the early days of the organisation's existence the EUDCE bureaucrats regarded loyalty, compliance, innocence, responsibility, obedience and a misplaced sense of respect as signs of stupidity and weakness. They encouraged a sense of trust and then took advantage of the trust they had helped create and nurture. And as the months and years passed by, in something of a blur it has to be said, it became harder and harder for those who wanted to protest to do so.

The majority, the electorate who had given away power in

ignorance or misplaced allegiance, were weakened; oppressed by fear (deliberately exacerbated) and by endless, ever-changing, ever-thickening layers of bureaucracy; confused and frightened; strangled by red tape; always running and hiding from the unknown and from their own susceptibilities and inadequacies; always busy, too busy to speak out, too busy and afraid to put their heads above the parapet; too afraid to protest; sometimes, it seemed too busy to breathe. Official policy was, and had been for years, to scare people and to then solve their fears by offering to take responsibility. All the people had to do was to obey the rules they were given. EUDCE kept creating more enemies, more fear and more rules. It was as though the oxygen had been sucked out of the air in the same way that the goodness had been squeezed out of the food. The people were medicated, abused, poisoned, threatened, tortured and used. Always used. Always abused by cryptorchid lickspittles. In the end people just did their best to get by; to survive; and to forget.

Much of the time they did not understand what was happening to them. And much of the time, it seemed, they simply did not care as long as there was the Telescreen to provide pseudo-spiritual and quasi-intellectual balm.

Chapter 5

The credit crunch which started in 2007 as a result of a peculiarly potent mixture of greed, corruption, dishonesty and incompetence (spread widely and generously among politicians, bankers, economists and civil servants) was so badly managed that it led to the world's first major financial crisis. What was at the time called the United Kingdom was at the epicentre. Thanks to the exaggerated nature of the greed and incompetence among British politicians and bankers the nation stumbled and then fell. Interest rates eventually hit 20%, paused for a while and then soared; inflation rose so high that the officials entrusted with the job of massaging the official figures gave up and stopped even trying to estimate the rate at which prices were rising; the pound sterling collapsed as rapidly as the German deutschmark and the Zimbabwean dollar had done before it. Politicians who had been in power during the early part of the 21st century fled abroad to escape the wrath of a furious electorate.

The UK's energy shortage, a consequence of an absence of planning that would have mortified a half-competent housewife, was intensified by the collapse in the world's supply of commodities. Richer countries took most of what there was. Not being one of the richer countries, very little oil or gas found its way to Britain. Food shortages were so severe that starvation and malnutrition overtook cancer and heart disease as the commonest causes of death.

The EU's policies had for years encouraged waste, pollution and almost irreparable environmental damage, with the result that domestic food production had fallen, fallen and fallen again. The lack of oil, and the consequent inability to import food supplies from other continents, meant dramatic and permanent food shortages. People had to queue for everything. Shopping for the ingredients for a simple meal would often take a morning. There were separate queues for individual vegetables so the shopper had to stand in line three times to buy potatoes, cabbages and beans. Then, there were queues to pay for the items and to collect a payment receipt. And, finally, more queuing to present the receipt and pick up the produce that had been paid for. It was, said one man, worse than buying a book at Foyles had been in the 1960s. A meal involving four ingredients meant standing in line twelve times.

With hardly noticed irony EUDCE announced that it would save the people of Europe from starvation (a problem caused almost entirely by the EU's policies) by introducing a strict rationing policy, and by issuing food coupons to ensure the fair distribution of supplies. Naturally, the food coupons were issued in large quantities to the sprouts and in very small quantities to the suspects.

It wasn't just food supplies that were severely constrained. Non-food purchases had to be made from charity shops (pretty much the only shops available) the majority of which received their stock in shipments from a number of Asian countries, mainly the two richest nations: China and India.

Shortages and rationing applied only to suspects. Sprouts were allowed to shop at special stores where food was available in unlimited quantities at token prices. For suspects, all foods were strictly rationed and shoppers had to accept whatever they were given when they got to the front of the relevant queue, even though the vegetables they were given might be bruised and half-rotten. Attempts to cheat the system and avoid queues by forming syndicates to buy food were regarded as a serious offence. Offenders who were caught were treated as guilty, because it was quicker and generally considered better all round for the community, and summarily deported without a trial.

There were street protests, of course. But, thanks to the mass of wide-ranging and oppressive anti-terror legislation introduced by the EU and by Labour Party in the late 1990's and the early part of the 21st century, these were quickly crushed.

There was much mumbling and complaining but those who mumbled were fearful and most of their complaining was done behind closed doors. Doing the right thing, and expecting others to do it, was regarded as eccentric, childlike, naive and, most importantly, entirely futile. Originality, unpredictability and inconsistency were all regarded as 'bad'. And as people grew to expect corruption and oppression so their moral compasses became distorted and then stopped working completely. People wearily accepted the way things had become as the way things had to be.

As the world's supplies of oil and gas shrank, and as the United Kingdom's situation grew daily more precarious, the number of people leaving the country grew to unprecedented proportions. Many of the migrants who had come to the UK in response to the promises of free money, free health care and free everything else, headed back to where they'd come from. As the infrastructure crumbled so the population shrank and the country became increasingly weak and unable to defend itself. National Health Service hospitals, top heavy with expensive bureaucracy, closed in many parts of the country, leaving millions with no formal health care. The British Government's gilts were formally given junk bond status. British manufacturing industry had long ago died. Now it was the turn of the service industries. Most were driven to bankruptcy by EUDCE red tape, massively high energy costs and the inability to compete with competing service industries in Asia, South America and the eastern reaches of the new European Superstate; the United States of Europe. Only those providing services which could not readily be outsourced (plumbers, hairdressers, dentists) survived.

Thanks to the peculiar greed of its bankers and politicians the UK was the worst affected of any of the world's nations. The consistent failure of successive governments to devise an energy policy exacerbated the nation's problems. Not that the UK was the only country in Europe to fall into deep trouble. As China, India, Russia, Brazil and other rapidly developing countries expanded and grew richer so European countries became increasingly unable to afford commodities.

The Chinese stockpiled everything worth having (oil, steel, uranium, gold and copper) leaving the USA and EUDCE to cope as best as they could without. Those countries such as Australia and Canada which were rich in natural resources prospered but the Eastern European countries and Ireland, Italy, Spain and Greece had tumbled into an ever-tightening circle of depression and despair. Eventually, even France and Germany were dragged down.

When what was then still the European Union offered loans and subsidies (more of the former than the latter) the money was accepted with alacrity. There were strings galore, of course, but neither desperate politicians nor what was left of the Bank of England had the inclination or the strength to take too much notice of them. The EU already had much power in Britain, of course. At the end of the 20th century, and in the early years of the 21st century, a series of British Prime Ministers had signed away more and more of the nation's diminishing independence. When Gordon Brown signed the Lisbon Treaty he was willingly handing over the final shreds of sovereignty to the commissioners and commissars in Brussels. Since that signing the European Union had taken over completely. The Government had obediently done everything it was told to do. It had destroyed rural communities by closing down local hospitals and small post offices. It had made it impossible for the children of poor families to rise in the world by introducing increasingly onerous student loans.

The Government had replaced freedom and democracy with statism and centralised power; the malevolent consequence of a potent mixture of communism, socialism, fascism and paternalism; the identical quadruplets who tear away responsibility, accountability, integrity and identity and replace them with rules, regulations and unfettered, unquestioned, unquestionable authority.

Like the governments of other signatory nations the British Government had privatised the post offices, police forces, bureaucratic institutions and armed forces. And then the EU had closed the British Parliament and transferred every scrap of power to Brussels and to the Regional Authorities. And then EUDCE was born. The devil child of the devil parent.

The new Europe was by then already more statist than Russia or China had been back in the 1970's. What had once been Britain had become a statist subunit of the new EUDCE; a world in which central planning was run by a series of fat controllers who decided how much corn should be grown, how much bread should be baked and how much of what the fat controllers hadn't eaten should be consumed by the proletariat, and how much should be sold to under-developed countries to make sure that their farmers didn't make a living and put the agricultural export business on the slide. The world of EUDCE was a world with as much charm and flexibility as a painting by numbers kit. (The fact that central planning had failed dismally in China and the USSR did not discourage the supporters of EUDCE from giving it a go.)

And then, when people no longer had any money with which to buy all the stuff the Chinese were churning out (flat screen television sets, complicated motor cars for which there was no petrol and gym shoes costing as much as a good suit with hand stitched lapels and four horn buttons on each cuff) China suddenly found itself with stockpiles of these things. And so Chinese entrepreneurs, who were just beginning to enjoy their taste of capitalism, went bust and the financial merry-go-round stopped turning and suddenly there wasn't enough money to pay people who were sick or retired and only enough to pay people who worked for EUDCE, the only layer of political authority which had the power to lay its fat, white hands on what little money was left.

Since EUDCE's regional parliaments, and their administrative substructures, had completely replaced individual sovereign parliaments, and inevitably their civil service administrations, those who had previously worked for individual governments or local bodies had all been made redundant, given resettlement gratuities in lieu of pensions and invited to apply for posts within EUDCE. The lucky ones, the chosen ones, the ones with contacts and relatives already working within the European Union, had been given EUDCE employment status. When an internal survey showed that 98% of new hirings were related to, or closely linked to, existing employees the response of those who commissioned the survey was to ask just why the other 2% had been hired. Jobs had been allocated according to a Positive Reformation Preferential System designed to ensure that the most important posts were allocated to citizens from the three selected nations: France, Germany and Turkey. The unlucky ones, the majority, had been demoted to habitant or suspect status and employed on short-term contracts with no security, no pensions, no status and no rights. The Turks got what they thought were the best jobs, of course, though the French managed to keep many of the really powerful jobs for themselves. The French had made a move for control of EUDCE when Turkey's membership had weakened Britain and Germany (alone among the main countries that made up EUDCE the French had refused to allow the Turks entry to their country). German politicians threatened to take their region out of EUDCE ('we were never really in', they claimed). French became EUDCE's second official language and even the lowest sprouts now tried to speak it. (The former British citizens, having an inborn inability to speak foreign languages, spoke something referred to as pidgin franglais.) Turkish had, of course, become the official language of EUDCE though no one but the Turks spoke or understood much of that.

Colourless, unimaginative bureaucrats, uninspired and uninspiring, appointed en masse by power hungry commissars, spread tanker loads of public money to enrich their relatives and to purchase loyalty. The commissars knew that, like dogs obedient to their masters, those they empowered would support to the death those who gave them their fat salaries, their index-linked pensions and, most of all, their authority (none of which they could have ever hoped to acquire fairly, decently or justly). Empowered by a state bureaucracy and enriched and ever more emboldened by their new status, officials who had been merely relentlessly rude, deliberately obstructive and unendingly officious rose to new heights in all these areas. It was, for them, The Time and they much enjoyed it.

None of the bureaucrats had any experience of the world that you cannot get sitting in a first class train seat paid for by the taxpayers or eating in five star hotel restaurants (while attending conferences paid for by taxpayers). They had no experience at all of real life, and they wanted none. Their predecessors had at least taken holidays with those of the real world. No more did they do this. The EU bureaucrats back in the early years of the 21st century had to queue in NHS hospitals like real people. The NHS staff had to queue at the airport just like ordinary people. But no more. The sprouts had acquired, been given, taken, privileges. They lived exceptional lives, protected at all costs from the vagaries of the real world. Sprouts never had to apologise. They were never disciplined. The system existed for them. They were the lords of all.

It took a time for suspects to realise that things had changed.

For a while, some people continued to assume that sprouts were there to serve; to make things better for the community, for 'ordinary' working people, to fight for a better society. The more uppity suspects liked to think that the sharp-tongued, rude, aggressive civil servants who worked at airports and railway stations and hospitals were an exception, rather than the rule; rule-happy, uniformed bullies who simply enjoyed the authority they'd taken and found that they rather liked.

But gradually it became clear that the bureaucrats had become officious, overbearing and arrogant by default. They weren't there to serve the community. They worked, they existed, with one purpose in mind: to further their own ends, to extend their power and their status and their wealth. The suspects were the drones. The sprouts were the queens. It took the people some time to realise this. But it was the way. It was the truth.

The new EUDCE offered aid and assistance to the regions. But EUDCE's assistance, which included financial support and access to EUDCE's own centrally managed stocks and supplies of oil, gas, coal, uranium and other essential commodities was, inevitably, conditional. The result was that EUDCE, which already had complete power in principle had, for the first time, complete power in practice.

Advice and financial support from the International Monetary Fund was summarily rejected so that power could remain in Brussels and Strasbourg. The media, controlled and manipulated (through a sophisticated and effective mixture of threats and bribery) said nothing that was not approving. The mass of people, fearful and gullible, greeted EUDCE's every involvement with gratitude and almost audible sighs of relief. Local administrations were replaced overnight by the unelected, undemocratic Regional Authorities which had for years been sitting quietly on the sidelines waiting for this very moment.

Europe had genuinely become a two-tier society – those who worked for the European Superstate and those who didn't. Most of the jobs within the Superstate were manufactured non-jobs, designed primarily to provide employment, salaries, and pension entitlements.

Some of the jobs created were absurd. Tom had heard of one man employed as a Nasal Passage Obstructive Materials Extraction Supervising Trainee. He spent his days teaching children how to blow their noses. And there were two dozen Senior Presentation Manipulation Officers at the Lard Information Council.

Nepotism was at its most perfect within the European Commission. In the bad old days the commissioners had been appointed by national governments. The demise of national governments meant that such appointments inevitably came to an end. In the new EUDCE the 100 permanent commissioners (known by State decree as Princes) were allowed to pass their titles on either to their children or to the appointee of their choice.

By the end of its first frantic week of existence the new EUDCE had hired all the staff it needed. The millions of former civil servants who had been made redundant were denied redundancy payments on the grounds that their employer, various parts of the United Kingdom Government, no longer existed and could not, therefore, be expected to honour what had long been regarded as commitments. Their pensions, once considered to be gold-plated, disappeared overnight.

Private Pension funds which had been regarded as inviolable became 'legacy assets'. Billions of pounds worth of investments suddenly became billions of euros worth of debts. Millions who had thought themselves among the most securely positioned in the country, suddenly found themselves without any visible means of support and without any prospects. Trade unions which protested that this was against the law were outlawed. The UK no longer existed, said EUDCE, and so its obligations had disappeared with it.

Two men in the North of England were deported after covering up EUDCE flags on motor car number plates with England flags. A couple in Dorchester were deported after a Union Jack, neatly ironed and folded, was found at the back of a wardrobe in their bedroom. A man in a public house in Taunton was deported after making a joke about EUDCE. Nowhere else in Europe were individuals persecuted with such enthusiasm and venom as they were hunted down in England. The eurocrats knew just how dangerous the English could be. England had been, they knew, the home of the Magna Carta, habeas corpus and Chaucer. It was the birthplace of William Shakespeare, John Milton and Winston Churchill, Isaac Newton and Robert Stevenson. It was the homeland of Lord Byron and William Blake, Charles Darwin and Charles Dickens. England had given the world Samuel Johnson, James Watt, Michael Faraday, Edward Jenner, John Keats and Christopher Wren, Oliver Cromwell, Charles Babbage, William Harvey and Joseph Lister, John Dalton, Queen Elizabeth I, Francis Bacon and Thomas Malthus. No other country had given the world one half the number of inventions that the English had given. And England was the universally recognised birthplace of parliamentary democracy. It was the birthplace too, of industry, finance, business and just about every sport on the planet.

And, most important of all, although the English are always slow to rise, and always reluctant revolutionaries, they were known within EUDCE to be the most determined, most bloody-minded people on earth. Bulldogs. Terriers.

The founders of EUDCE knew that if their project was to succeed, to bloom, they had to destroy England, demoralise the English, ruthlessly eradicate English culture and suppress all memory of

English history. And they had to stamp on any sign of burgeoning English revolutionary zeal.

There were some protests, of course. But the leaders were quickly arrested and passed on, via the Americans, to other nations. (The words 'suspected', 'arrested', 'charged' and 'sentenced' had become synonymous, as had 'intent' and 'guilt'.) Torture and imprisonment had been outsourced. The bureaucrats said it made economic sense and there was no one to dispute their saying. They called it the deleveraging of progress, though no one really knew what that meant. Anyone who opposed or criticised the peaceful work of EUDCE, the European Superstate (formerly known as the EU, EC, ECC and the Common Market) was officially defined as a terrorist.

They used fear to keep everyone in line; they had found the real power of intellectual terrorism. When terror triumphs it is institutionalised and thus it was.

Chapter 6

If you weren't a registered, licensed sprout then jobs were hard to come by.

As a white male suspect Tom was not allowed to vote, own a motor car, have oil tokens or take any sort of permanent, full-time work. As a result Tom worked part time as a cobbler. Repairing shoes kept him busy. No one could afford to buy new ones. Even if they had been able to afford new ones there were no shoes shops. And if there had been any shoe shops there were no shoes for them to sell. Cobbling was a good business to be in. He didn't have a shop, of course. Most of the few shops remaining were charity shops. He worked at home. Sometimes, if there were enough shoes to mend, he would go to someone's home and repair them there.

He also had, and was grateful for, a steady private job as an allotment guard. He worked every Wednesday from 6 p.m. to 12 p.m. at the Sub-Region 47/H298 Community Growth Project. The allotment had once been a graveyard, but being centrally placed and having good soil meant that it had been compulsorily purchased. The gravestones had been torn out and dumped in a huge pile in one corner of the graveyard. There had been a plan to use the broken pieces of stone to repair crumbling buildings but no one had ever got round to putting the plan into action. Now people grew their own vegetables in the graveyard and Tom had been hired by the allotment holders as a guard to make sure that the hungry and the homeless did not succeed if they were weak enough to succumb to temptation and strong enough to do something about it. (The appointment had, of course, been confirmed and approved by the South Eastern Regional Parliamentary Commission.)

Tom was lucky to have the work together with the pay packet, and the occasional handful of food that he could earn if he did small jobs for the allotment holders. There was no job security, of course and if he was too ill to attend he didn't get paid. Only sprouts had job security, sick pay, pensions and employment rights.

He dreamt of producing a small newsletter, an independent source of news for suspects. But it was impossible to find a printing machine or a paper supply and so the dream remained a dream. But he kept it alive. 'What is a man without his dreams?' he asked himself whenever the dream began to fade.

Chapter 7

Having a sprout on the doorstep was a frightening enough thought. Having one actually in the house was close enough to alarming to have given Tom palpitations. Tom looked around upstairs, desperately trying to see his world through the eyes of a sprout. The first thing he noticed was a battered paperback copy of David Copperfield lying beside the bed. He grabbed it, and quickly skimmed it under the bed so that it was out of sight. Not even sprouts were allowed to read Dickens any more.

Dickens was an English author and, therefore, like Shakespeare and others of that nationality, officially proscribed. Conquering England, and turning it into nine regions, had been the most difficult task for the EUDCE bureaucrats. It was something of which they were particularly proud. They had for years run a clever propaganda war to outlaw Englishness. They'd fired up hatred of the English among the Scots and the Welsh by telling extraordinary lies about historical events. It had been very effective.

'I'm a Senior Soft Artefacts Label Inspector,' said the newcomer. He looked to be in his early 40s – young enough to be enthusiastic and not old enough to have lost his enthusiasm for his job or his belief in the organisation. He liked to sound polite and helpful when he first met suspects. He felt that politeness, unexpected and out of context, was always curiously menacing. Underneath the fake courtesy he had the same confidence enjoyed by all the sprouts. Like most petty officials his self-importance was derived from the knowledge that he, and not the suspect to whom he was talking, had access to really important people.

Boris Perovskite was short and clinically obese and a fully trained expert on Label Maintenance Legislation. No one had used his first name for at least a decade. He was Romanian and homosexual. Recruiters always gave priority to applicants who were born outside the country where they were working. And they were instructed to give preferential treatment to applicants who were not heterosexual. (Applicants of both sexes who had not undergone the quasi-compulsory homosexual 'experience' at one of the Gay Awareness Camps, widely regarded as EUDCE's version of National

Service, were not entitled to be considered for any sort of official post.)

Perovskite had three interests: his moustache (which he trimmed each morning so that it looked as much like Adolf Hitler's as possible), his collection of 1970's Japanese music boxes and his work. He attended compulsory body-realignment tutorials three afternoons a week and counselling sessions two evenings a week. At the tutorials he was encouraged to discuss his interest in food with a trained nutritionist who believed that talking about food would eventually reduce Perovskite's addiction to chips and burgers. At the counselling sessions Perovskite was encouraged to talk about his obsession with food to a trained and qualified counsellor who had an open mind on all issues and was concerned only with offering support. Because Perovskite insisted on the sessions being conducted in his native language, and because there was a shortage of Romanian nutritionists and counsellors, translators were hired to attend all these sessions. Since the course of tutorials and counselling sessions had begun Perovskite had gained just 17 kilograms in weight. Computer generated graphs showed that his weight was accumulating at a slower pace than before the sessions had started and so both the nutritionist and the counsellor had received substantial bonuses from EUDCE as a reward for this success.

Perovskite checked the soles of his shoes before entering Tom's home. He checked not, as most people do, to make sure that his shoes were clean but to make sure that they were dirty. He always stepped in dog faeces before performing a domestic inspection. It gave him a buzz to walk around leaving a stinking trail on the carpets and his work always took him into every room in a house. No one ever complained. No one ever complained about sprouts. If suspects were young, male, attractive and alone he always insisted that they remove all their clothes, including approved undergarments, so that he could check that the labels had not been tinkered with. Being a Software Label Inspector was so much more fun than being a Hardware Label Inspector. Who wanted to look at the backs of fridges and Telescreen sets all day long?

'Under EUDCE Directive 4879/28162 I have the authority to...' Tom's brain shut down temporarily. A Soft Artefacts Label Inspector was, he knew, authorised to enter any suspect's home to check that EUDCE approval and rating labels had not been removed from furniture, duvets and other bed linen, carpets, soft toys and clothing.

The law said that A&R labels, as they were known, had to be at least 4 cm by 4 cm in size. They were usually bigger. And somehow, they almost managed to look unsightly. On clothing, particularly underclothing, they were often placed in a position that seemed designed to cause maximum discomfort. The penalty for removing a EUDCE approved rating label was severe.

'Do you understand?' demanded the second inspector, as though speaking to a slightly backward child.

Pierogi Tchotchke was sweating and had clearly been doing so for some time for he smelt of stale sweat. He was shaped like a pear and had a long, thinnish face that made him look a little like a badger, though he did not look as sensitive, as friendly or as intelligent as a badger. He was 22-years-old and reputed to be the youngest Soft Artefacts Labels Inspector in the region. He did not consider himself to be a dull, one-track person like many of his colleagues. (He regarded Perovskite as dull and superficial and it irked him that Perovskite was the senior Inspector and would occasionally make this clear to the suspects whose artefacts they were inspecting.) Tschotchke boasted of having a number of interests outside his work. He collected pocket calculators and had over a hundred of them. He was also contemplating starting a collection of commercial adding machines. When required to give a preference (on forms and when making purchases in the sprout stores) he always stated that he was heterosexual, though he had not, as yet, acquired any experience in this area.

The thick, dark blue suits they both wore had been designed to be hard wearing and warm in winter. Female sprouts wore the same sort of suits. As he looked at the two sprouts in their ghastly suits Tom couldn't help thinking of Thoreau's advice that we distrust any enterprise that requires new clothes. How Thoreau would have distrusted the European Superstate. The material of which the suits were made was said to be waterproof and quite possibly was. But it wasn't the right sort of thing to be wearing in midsummer. The suits were both worn and shiny. Numerous snags and darns showed that the stuff of which the suits were made wasn't as hard-wearing as the manufacturers claimed. Lower grade sprouts received one new suit a year and so they had to wear the same suit every day. Since the only dry cleaning shops dealt exclusively with the clothes of high level sprouts, and since the material took a day or more to dry out if washed, the sprouts rarely, if ever, washed their suits. They weren't paid well enough to buy other clothes so they wore their official-issue suits every day, whether they were working or not. It was hardly surprising that they all stank.

Tom nodded.

'Sign here.' Aggressively, quite rudely, Tchotchke thrust a paper pad towards Tom who took it, read it, scribbled his signature on it and handed it back.

The inspectors had once used electronic signature pads. They'd gone back to paper records for two reasons. Repeated and unexpected outages in wireless communication systems had resulted in the loss of masses of collected data. And restrictions in supplies of raw materials meant that replacing the portable electronic devices had proved impossible, even for EUDCE. Not even EUDCE could get hold of portable computers. The oil shortage meant that there were no longer any factories capable of making them. And even if there had been there wouldn't have been any batteries for them. The authorities still kept computerised web-based records but only on network linked desk-top hardware. Unlike everyone else EUDCE did still have an almost reliable electricity supply.

'How many people are there sharing this accommodation?' demanded Perovskite. In the old days the sprouts always knew the answers before they asked the questions. Since they'd had to revert to carrying paper forms they'd lost their edge. These days they only knew if someone had lied when they got back to their headquarters and keyed in the information they'd been given. But all sprouts who met with suspects as part of their daily routine had extensive training in how to dominate conversations with posture and tone of voice. They were like policemen, army officers and headmasters in that they knew how to demand attention and respect. It had been decided by EUDCE's Citizen Manipulation Advisors (of whom there were many) that calling EUDCE employees 'officiers', and everyone else suspects was an easy way to establish an automatic pecking order; to give EUDCE employees status and to make everyone else feel suspicious, vulnerable and, most important of all, defensive.

'Three,' replied Tom, who found himself feeling curiously apologetic; as though he had been caught doing something wrong before the interrogation had even started. 'Myself, my wife and my aunt.'

'Still living with auntie, eh?' sneered the inspector, writing down this information on the pad. He wrote slowly, deliberately, with the tip of his tongue sticking out of his mouth. Tom noticed that he used the stub of a green colouring pencil. This wasn't for any particular reason. There was a worldwide shortage of pens and EUDCE had commandeered every writing implement they could find. Some sprouts were filling in forms with charcoal sticks, others were using children's crayons. Filling in the small spaces on the forms with thick crayons was notoriously difficult.

'She's suffering from Alzheimer's disease,' explained Tom. 'We took her in. She is too old and too ill for institutional care. And she's a suspect, of course.'

The inspector looked at Tom. 'You think the policy of protecting the State's facilities for essential employees is a bad one?' Even in speech he somehow managed to give the word 'State' the dignity of an initial capital letter.

'No, no, not at all,' lied Tom quickly. Lying came easy to everyone when talking to sprouts. Tom consoled himself with the thought that the truth is often a complicated confection of contradictions. Nothing is ever as simple or as straightforward as we would like it to be. The one relevant certainty was that criticising EUDCE policy was illegal and was an offence which was taken very seriously. It was for this reason that no one in Government or the media had ever been able to blame EUDCE for the closure of post offices, the chronic and accelerating shortage of GPs, the deterioration in schools, the abandoning of weekly rubbish collections (and, subsequently, the abandonment of fortnightly collections and, eventually, the complete abandonment of rubbish collections), the disappearance of long-established army regiments, the disappearance of policemen from the streets and so on and so on.

The result was that the EUDCE laws were adhered to strictly, regardless of whether or not they made any sort of sense. And laws were the one thing that wasn't in short supply. Each EUDCE Commissioner thought he was the only one making rules (and creating chaos). But there were 100 commissioners – all making rules and causing chaos. The rules just kept coming; fluttering into people's lives like snowflakes. Endless nonsense which seemed designed to destroy every sensible aspect of human endeavour. Much of the red tape was conflicting. So, for example, there was a law which said that bicycles should all be equipped with two bells (one to use and one as a spare in case the other one didn't work) and another that said that ringing a bicycle bell was unacceptable noise pollution. The result was that bicycles were all fitted with two bells but no one ever rang any of them (except by accident). Applicants taking the examination for their bicycle riding licence (just about every human activity, including sex, required a licence and, inevitably, a test fee and an annual maintenance fee) were expected to display their ability to use their bells without actually ringing them.

There was a law (introduced by the Muslim Affairs Commissioner) which said that women should cover their heads whenever they went out in public. And there was another law (introduced by a lobbyist representing a group of Jews) which stated firmly that it was illegal for women to cover their heads.

Whatever you did could get you arrested and deported. Tweedledum and Tweedledee, the Red Queen and the Mad Hatter would have all felt at home in the United States of Europe.

'You have permission for her to be living here?'

Tom nodded. 'We were granted permission.'

'And you pay the fee for a Residential Aunt Licence?'

Tom nodded.

The inspector painstakingly wrote all this down on his form. The sprouts always worked slowly. There were too many of them and they tried to spread out their work so that it didn't quite fit the time available. It was, they knew, the best way to ensure they weren't made redundant. Very few sprouts were ever made redundant but it was the one thing that terrified them. Falling from sprout to suspect meant losing everything: dignity, status, income, pension rights, shopping privileges, health care rights and transport access. (It had been said, by a former Bishop, now lost somewhere in Africa, that suspects were treated worse than black folk had been treated in America's deep south. 'To be a suspect in 21st century Europe is to be a nigger,' he had announced in his last sermon, noting that suspects were not allowed to use any form of public transport designated for use by sprouts.)

Very occasionally the authorities would make an example of someone 'pour encourager les autres'. The dismissed sprouts were always lowly functionaries, of course. Higher-ranking employees had guaranteed jobs, pensions and perks for life.

The sprout looked around, taking in the threadbare carpet, the lumpiness of the two easy chairs and the sofa and the shabbiness of the other furniture. The magazines neatly lined up on the coffee table were well-read. The date on the magazine on the top of the pile showed that it was 14-years-old. There was a small bookcase against one wall. 'You've a lot of rubbish in here, haven't you?' He walked over to the bookcase, turned his head to one side and read the titles to check that they were all on the approved list.

***

Tom wasn't worried. He knew that the books on display were all licensed. Most of them were EUDCE publications glorifying the European State's magnificent history, and the many ways in which it had enriched the lives of the European people. Despite having published a number of books of its own EUDCE didn't really approve of books and had slapped a huge tax on anything published by outsiders, in order to discourage reading. The American CIA had once produced a report showing that books encourage people to think and thereby encourage more revolutionary activity than newspapers, radio and television put together. EUDCE agreed with this. They had issued a statement announcing that all revolutions and 'bad thoughts' were started by books and that in future adults should derive most of their entertainment and education from officially blessed (and licensed) programmes broadcast on the Telescreen by the BBC.

In the last days of schools, just before cereal manufactures were licensed to give away free diplomas, primary school children who attended at least once a week were automatically given a degree in anything they could spell. Tom knew children aged 12 who had so many degrees that it took them ten minutes to write them all down. Children under six years of age went not to infant school but to pre-university college. Talk that EUDCE had lowered standards was dismissed as nonsense. A bureaucrat who had just awarded a fistful of degrees to a four-year-old Latvian, said that the evidence proved conclusively that standards had been raised. But there had been an outcry when an eighteen-month-old Israeli had been shown on the Telescreen receiving his 100th degree (during the ceremony the recipient stuck it into his mouth and ate a good part of it).

Now children no longer went to school ('What is the point of wasting public money on building schools when every child already has its own personal tutor?' demanded a leading sprout, a licensed educationalist, explaining why children should obtain all their education from the Internet. 'We should not waste money on such fripperies as schools.')

When schools had closed, the Telescreen had been the only source of educational material. Lessons were available on the BBC and examinations were also taken and marked on the Telescreen. A survey Tom had seen on the BBC had reported that 98% of children under 10 had chosen to specialise in studying celebrity gossip and advanced celebrity gossip. Just over 96% of older students were taking degrees in similar subjects.

('My 14-year-old has just completed a PhD on political gossip from the early 21st century,' a friend of Tom's had told him. 'She can tell you endless stuff about all sorts of people I've never heard of. She knows more than is decent to know about some woman called Jordan who was apparently a Regional Health Minister for a while, a transsexual called Simone Cowell who was a Regional Foreign Secretary for a year and two broadcasters called Ross and Brand. The Jordan woman was apparently appointed Regional Health Minister because of her experience of cosmetic surgery. Sadly, it all ended tragically. She apparently suffered a melt-down during a particularly hot summer. Ross and Brand were apparently well-known in their day, though I haven't the foggiest what they did. They apparently both ended up presenting home decorating programmes on a Do It Yourself channel that ran for a while a few years ago. Back in the days when there were lots of channels. And, if you're really interested, my 14-year-old has a friend who can tell you the bowel habits of at least sixty reality television stars.' Tom had gratefully declined the offer.) The enthusiasm for webucation programmes (as they were called) had been severely damaged by the introduction of supermarket degrees. Sprouts and suspects alike could obtain educational qualifications merely by joining the approved 'Free Degrees Programme' on the Telescreen and collecting coupons issued by the googletesco, EUDCE's official online store.

Tom and Dorothy Cobleigh had a neighbour whose 5-year-old daughter, Enid, although illiterate and innumerate, had already collected degrees in advanced mathematics and Telescreen appreciation. The most popular degree course was in The History of Nail Varnish Application Technology. (Sadly, suspects couldn't buy nail varnish even if they had the money. The few small manufacturers supplied only stores which were available only to sprouts.)

***

Tom didn't say anything. Sprouts always liked to sneer.

'Why isn't the screen switched on?' demanded the inspector, indicating the screen on the wall above the fireplace. The sprouts didn't miss anything. Suspects were supposed to have their screens switched on all the time so that they could watch the BBC whenever they were at home. Public places were all fitted with Telescreens too.

For a while there had been a few pirate stations, broadcasting illegally from hidden sites, but they had quickly been closed down in the interests of free speech. Now the BBC was the only approved broadcaster and in practical terms that meant the only broadcaster. More hated than ever, no one called the organisation the Beeb or Auntie any more. No one felt fondly towards such an overtly propagandist organisation and no one trusted anything heard on the Telescreen. Suspects who wanted to know what was going on gleaned what information they could from rumours passed mouth to mouth and shared face to face. The rumours were sometimes accurate but more often they were not. Naturally, since no one knew whether what they were hearing was true or untrue this meant that everything they heard was as worthless as the information broadcast on the BBC.

The only way to access what had once been known as the Internet, was through the State-approved search engine, which blocked all unapproved sites and put EUDCE approved sites at the top of all searches. The quality and reliability of information available was so poor that most suspects wouldn't have bothered with it even if they had been able to afford reliable equipment or had a reliable electricity supply.

Sprouts were entitled to ask suspects questions about recent BBC news items. They were empowered to stop suspects in the street and ask five questions. Any suspect who scored less than 40% was given three penalty points on their roaming licence and required to be tested once a week on their knowledge of Telescreen topics. Accumulate twelve penalty points and your roaming licence was automatically endorsed and you weren't allowed to leave home without passing a new citizenship examination. Tom knew people who hadn't been out of their homes for years.

Roaming licences (the successors to identity cards) had been made compulsory soon after the Treaty of Lisbon was extended by the commissioners. (The Treaty of Lisbon had given the European Union complete power to introduce new laws. It had been the end of British sovereignty.) The roaming licences had to be renewed annually. There was, of course, a charge.

'It is turned on but the community windmill has stopped working again so we have no electricity,' explained Tom. 'It's the fourth time this week.'

'Your community windmill has broken down?' The sprout made it sound as though it was Tom's fault.

Tom pointed to the window, through which stale, warm air drifted very slowly. There was no glass in the window and the old shower curtain which they used to keep out the rain and snow had been pulled to one side. The predominant smell in the room was of woodsmoke. Despite the heat there were stoves and fires burning in many of the homes in the area. There was no other way to heat water or to cook food. 'There's no wind,' he explained.

'Don't you have battery back ups?'

'No.'

'No grid support?'

'No.'

'You'll be on rationing here anyway.' It was a boast rather than a question. Only the gated communities where sprouts lived enjoyed constant electricity supplies. It really wasn't difficult to understand why sprouts were so loyal to EUDCE. If a sprout lost his job he had to move out of the gated community and into the 'real' world outside.

The sprout moved towards the narrow staircase.

'Where's the gate?' He pointed to the top of the staircase.

'Ah,' said Tom. 'The gate.'

'EUDCE Health and Safety Regulation HS9547/726,' said the sprout, pleased to have found fault so easily. 'Every intradwelling staircase containing more than three riser treads must be fitted with a gate at the top of the most elevated portion of the staircase and a safety harness, with approved guidance system, should be available for anyone ascending or descending the staircase.'

'The approved gates and harnesses are very expensive,' said Tom.

Smirking with satisfaction, the sprout made a note in his notebook and then, climbing very gingerly, headed up towards the first floor.

'We should get danger money for jobs like this,' he muttered, loudly enough for Tom to hear.

Chapter 8

Later, when it was all over and what had happened had become the past instead of the future, people often asked how it all started; how the Revolution began. The truth is, of course, that it is always a straw that breaks the camel's back. And straws always appear to be small, insignificant things.

They were on the landing at the top of the stairs.

'I need to inspect every item of bedding and every item of clothing,' said Perovskite. 'How many bedrooms do you have?'

'Two medium sized ones and a very small one,' replied Tom.

'Three,' said the sprout, writing this down in his notebook.

'One of them is very small. Hardly big enough to take a bed. It's what used to be called a box room.'

'Three bedrooms,' insisted the sprout. 'You and your wife sleep together?'

'Yes.'

'And your aunt has a room of her own?'

'Yes.'

'So you have a bedroom lying empty?'

'It's a very small room,' insisted Tom. 'We just keep junk in it.'

'If you have junk it should be sent for recycling,' said Tchotchke.

'Yes, of course.'

'I will send round a Residential Placement Officer,' said Perovskite. 'We will arrange for someone to use that room. Maybe a couple or even a family.'

'It's a very small room!' insisted Tom. 'Would you like to look at it? Please take a look, and you will see how small it is.' He opened the door to the third bedroom. It was dark inside. The glass in the window had been broken during the riots which had taken place five years earlier. It wasn't possible to buy glass so Tom and a friend called Keith had fixed up a metal screen at the window. The screen was made out of the flattened out roof of a Volkswagen. Keith spent his days chopping up unwanted vehicles and creating windows, doors and furniture out of them. With thousands of unwanted cars abandoned on the streets there was never any shortage of materials.

'There is no need for me to look,' snapped Perovskite who, like all his colleagues, found facts could be a nuisance. They had to be written down and stored and could get in the way afterwards. 'It is against the law to deprive fellow citizens of available accommodation.' As he spoke he punched a very podgy right forefinger into Tom's sternum. He punched so hard that Tom automatically backed away a little. 'Do you know the penalty?' He leant forwards to poke Tom again. 'The automatic penalty for a first offence is an increase in your tax rate. The penalty for a second offence is confiscation. What is your State tax rate at the moment?'

'Eighty per cent,' said Tom. Four fifths of any cash he and his wife Dorothy earned went straight to the State. They received no benefits and no allowances. English citizens had been taxed, taxed and taxed again to satisfy the ever-growing needs of EUDCE and, in particular, the weaker, poorer Eastern European regions which had joined EUDCE for the subsidies and grants they knew they would be entitled to claim. EUDCE's commissioners had welcomed these countries, despite the fact that they were likely to be a drain on the State for many years, for two reasons. First, because a bigger EUDCE gave those controlling it extra power. In the same way that company executives like to expand their companies because this gives them a good excuse to buy bigger jets and pay themselves more, so EUDCE bureaucrats wanted a larger State. And, secondly, because the introduction of new, poorer countries diminished the power of the older, more established nations such as France, Germany (and what was left of the United Kingdom).

Even before the administrative needs of EUDCE grew to mammoth proportions citizens had been taxed on their income, taxed on what they spent, taxed on what they saved or invested and taxed again when they had the effrontery to die. Now EUDCE was taxing people out of existence. Businesses all over the northern regions had been destroyed by high taxes and red tape and millions working in the private sector had given up official work and were taking small, part time jobs where they were often paid in kind rather than money. In the end all that was left was the red tape and the legions of tax collectors sitting around with nothing much to do.

The sprouts, meanwhile, were paying themselves more and more; giving one another increasingly extravagant expense accounts and huge bonuses for failure ('to help soothe the disappointment and guard against feelings of personal inadequacy it is essential to increase bonuses in times of departmental failure,' read the most significant report on the issue). And there were the index-linked pensions to be paid too.

Private enterprise had been bled to death and with the failure of non-state industries the basis of society had disappeared. Those who ran EUDCE, the insatiable monster, ever hungry for power and money, were blind to the problems and unable to see that when you kill the golden geese there are no more golden eggs.

'Your tax rate will go up immediately by another five per cent,' said the sprout. 'That's eighty five per cent.'

'I can't afford that,' protested Tom.

'That's your problem,' said the sprout smugly, with a careless shrug. He strode into the bedroom Tom shared with his wife. 'This is your bedroom?' Inside, he looked around. There wasn't much to see. A double bed. Two small bedside tables, each containing two drawers. A rickety wardrobe and a chest of drawers. 'These people don't realise how lucky they are to have us to make all their decisions for them,' Perovskite said to Tchotchke, speaking over Tom as though he wasn't there. The sprouts tended to do that a good deal. Perovskite strode across to the chest of drawers and tapped it on the top with his pad. 'What's in here?' he demanded.

'Clothes. Nightwear. A few jumpers. My underclothes. My wife's underclothes.'

The inspector opened a drawer. It contained two rather elderly jumpers. Both had holes in the sleeves and were frayed around the neck and cuffs. The sprout checked that the jumpers still had their labels, closed the drawer and opened the drawer to its left. It contained Dorothy's underwear: three brassieres, half a dozen pairs of knickers, two slips. They were all neatly folded but old and worn. Everything Tom and his wife owned was old and worn. The sprout picked out a brassiere and examined it carefully. 'She's a good size. Do you like women with big breasts?' He looked at Tom. Tom said nothing. Perovskite caressed the material for a moment, then examined the label and held it up.

'The label on this one still carries an old imperial measurement,' he said. '38D. That's inches!' He spat out the word 'inches' as though he didn't want it in his mouth for a moment more than was necessary.

'It's a very old bra,' explained Tom. 'But you'll see that the label also carries official EUDCE sizes.'

The inspector folded the brassiere and stuffed it into his pocket.

'This must go for recycling,' he said. 'As you should know it is an offence to possess clothing which still contains imperial measurements. They're a remnant of English imperialism.'

Tom said nothing. He cursed silently. Sprouts always looked for items carrying imperial measurements. It was the easy way for them to obtain convictions and to show that they were doing their jobs. An easy way for them to bully suspects. And an easy way for them to help themselves to valuable bits and pieces from people's homes. Anything which contained imperial measurements could be confiscated. Tom knew someone who had been arrested and deported for having a set of scales in his bathroom which still measured weight in pounds and stones. Such things were supposed to be burnt or otherwise destroyed after they'd been confiscated but everyone knew they weren't. The same people who had made a fortune confiscating and reselling expensive penknives while working at airports now made money confiscating, relabeling and reselling a whole range of illegal items. Even books which contained imperial measurements were confiscated and then resold on the black market.

Tchotchke pulled out another brassiere and examined the label on that one. He turned to Tom, smiled and put that into his pocket too. He didn't say anything.

Only one of the brassieres in Dorothy's drawer was legally acceptable. Obviously disappointed Tchotchke put that back into the drawer. 'Is she wearing a soutien-gorge today?' He used the French word for brassiere. Sprouts always used French words when they could, even if they didn't speak the language properly. It was an open sign of their loyalty to Brussels and their contempt for England and everything English. Tom had noticed that the British born sprouts were even more likely to use French words than the foreign born ones. And of the British born sprouts it was the Scots who were particularly likely to speak French whenever they could, though their mixture of accents meant that most of the time no one knew what they were trying to say. The Scots had become more bitter than ever when they had discovered that their Regional Parliament was merely a formal consequence of being a EUDCE region, rather than a prelude to the independence they thought they were going to be given.

'Yes, I think so. Yes, of course.'

'She must bring it into the Label offices for label inspection and authorisation or for confiscation.'

'She can't afford new bras,' said Tom. 'All our money goes on food and keeping the house warm during the winter.'

'Then she'll have to let her big boobies hang free won't she,' said Perovskite with a sneer. He went through the rest of the clothes and the bedding quite quickly. He confiscated a pair of Tom's trousers because the labels on them, though metric, were worn and almost unreadable, and three pairs of socks because they didn't have any labels at all.

'My socks have never had labels,' protested Tom.

'All items of clothing and soft furnishing must be labelled,' insisted Perovskite pompously. 'And it is an offence to remove or deface EUDCE approved labelling.' On the landing he turned and poked Tom in the chest again with his right forefinger. 'One way or another you're in quite a lot of trouble,' he said. Tchotchke snorted and sneered.

Tom didn't say anything. There was never any point in arguing with a sprout. The laws, and there were plenty of them, were always on their side. He suddenly remembered the slogan 'the customer is always right' from the 1950's. They'd effectively changed it to 'the sprout is always right'. Whole armies of people were employed solely to castigate, admonish, rebuke, reprove, berate and scold. Adults were treated like children and sprouts were treated like gods. It was widely accepted that the weight of a huge, intolerant and committed bureaucracy lay behind every order and every form, but the public voice was unheard. Every institutional demand, however meaningless and trivial, pointless and wrong-headed in concept, was carved in stone and delivered by truck. There was never room for dissent, discussion or such old-fashioned luxuries as logic and common sense. The mandarins and apparatchiks ruled and what, in a free society, might have grown into genuine, healthy, opposition had rotted and turned into a pustulant mess of resentments.

As Perovskite prodded again, Tom stepped backwards to get out of the way a little, and to minimise the pain of the poking. As he felt his foot dancing in mid-air he turned and saw that the stairs were directly behind him. He then half stumbled and half fell to one side in his attempt to prevent himself falling down the stairs. It was, in its way, an elegant pirouette.

Perovskite, still pushing forwards with his outstretched finger, suddenly found that there was nothing for him to push against. The chest he had intended to prod was no longer there to be prodded. He too stumbled, but instead of falling onto the landing he fell forwards, tripped over the outstretched legs of the fallen Tom and, with a shout and a great deal of noise, tumbled forwards and down the narrow stairs, bumping into the wall a good deal as he did so.

The second sprout, Tchotchke, rushed down after him, followed closely by Tom.

When Tom got to the bottom of the stairs he thought at first that Perovskite was dead. His eyes were closed and he was lying in a very uncomfortable looking way. But when Tom knelt down beside him and felt for a pulse in the man's neck he could feel the regular, rhythmic thump which told him that the man's heart was still beating strongly.

'Are you all right?' Tom asked, anxiously.

Slowly, the sprout opened his eyes and looked around him. 'I can't move my legs,' he said. He lifted his head a little. 'I can't move my hands.'

'Don't move,' said Tom. 'I'll ring for an ambulance.'

'Where is he going to move, you idiot,' demanded Tchotchke. 'And how? He's already told you that he can't move his arms or legs. Tell them who it's for.' The two-tier ambulance service, like all other State services, provided aid solely for sprouts.

Tom stood up, about to head for the front door. Suspects didn't have fixed line telephones but there was a telephone point less than a quarter of a mile away.

'You're going to fry for this,' Tchotchke hissed.

Puzzled, Tom paused. 'What do you mean?'

'You deliberately pushed him down the stairs!' said the sprout. 'They'll have you extradited to somewhere with the death penalty.'

'He *fell* down the stairs,' said Tom.

Tchotchke shook his head. 'No, he did not,' he said firmly. 'You pushed him' He turned 'pushed' into a two syllable word. He sneered at Tom. 'Of course I could be wrong,' he said. 'But it doesn't matter if I am, does it? So effectively I'm not.'

Tom knew that the sprout was right. Suspects who were charged with attacking sprouts were invariably sentenced to death. Under EUDCE law, suspects were not allowed to give evidence in their own defence.

To get round the fact that EUDCE didn't allow prisoners to be executed the sprouts regularly arranged for people they wanted executed to be transferred to less finicky parts of the world. With the help of the Americans, some went to Saudi Arabia, some to China and others to the United States of America itself where executions had become the most popular daily reality show on the American Telescreen.

'But it was an accident,' protested Tom.

The sprout managed a snort. 'You'll die for this. I'll see to it. Now go and get help. I'll stay with him.'

'It really wasn't my fault!' said Tom.

'You pushed him.'

'No, no, I didn't. He fell.'

Tchotchke looked at him. He didn't care about Tom and he didn't care about the crippled sprout lying on the floor. 'You will be executed,' he said firmly.

Tom hurried out of the front door, heading for the nearest telephone kiosk. Once there he put a coin into the box and dialled the number for medical emergencies. All emergency phone calls within EUDCE had been outsourced. Calls for what had been known as the police (and, although usually referred to as Europol, was now known as the European Defence and Public Protection Regulatory Force) went to a call centre in Germany, calls for fire services (now known as the European Conflagration Control Force) went to Poland and calls for lifeboat services (the European Maritime and Littoral Patrol Force) went to Lithuania. Calls for medical emergencies went to a telephone answering system in Italy. The reason for this was simple: the four Regions concerned had each offered the best price. The efficiency of the various systems had never been considered and the complications inevitably bound to ensue when emergency phone calls were answered by people who didn't speak the same language, let alone understand the geography or culture of the nation from which the call emanated, had never been regarded as of any significance. In practice, the result of all these changes was that in practice, and as far as ordinary citizens were concerned, there were no effective public services.

***

A few years earlier Tom had telephoned for the police when a neighbour, a former writer of cheap thrillers, had threatened to run amok with an axe. ('I'm going to run amok with an axe,' had been his exact words. It was the only time anyone had ever heard the word 'amok' used outside a newspaper or a courtroom.) The conversation on the telephone had been conducted in a mixture of languages. A word or two of German, a word or two of French, a word or two of Turkish (only just then the official language of EUDCE) and a word or two of English.

'Were you deprived or abused as a child?' asked the operator who eventually answered Tom's call.

'No, not particularly,' admitted Tom who had been through this sort of interrogation before. 'Though I didn't get a bicycle when Neville Bartholomew got one and I felt aggrieved about that for years. To be honest it still rankles. He had a red one with lots of gears.' He had found that if you did not answer the questions fully the interrogation tended to last much longer. The questioners always liked to be able to fill in their forms.

'Are you ethnic?'

'What exactly do you mean by that these days?' asked Tom.

'Were you born outside the country in which you now reside?'

'No.'

'Were your parents born out of the country in which you now reside?'

'No.'

'Is English your first language?'

'Yes, it is,' admitted Tom, who knew in his heart that this was the 'wrong' answer. 'I expect you're now going to ask me if any of my relatives make objects d'art out of used gourd skins?'

The telephone operator sounded puzzled. There was a long pause as he looked at the screen in front of him. 'That's not on my list of questions,' he said at last.

'So, can you send someone round?' asked Tom. 'This guy is about to run amok.'

'Has he threatened any persons of ethnic origin?'

'Not yet. But there's a Welsh guy living upstairs. He could be in the line of fire pretty soon.'

'We'll send someone round but it will probably be next Wednesday.'

'Morning or afternoon?'

'I'm afraid I can't tell you that for security reasons.'

***

The telephone rang and rang and rang. Eventually, Tom heard a voice. But it was, as Tom had expected, a recorded voice.

'This is the national telephone line for medical emergencies,' said a calm, female voice speaking first in heavily accented French and then repeating the initial message in German, Spanish and English. The woman who had recorded the message then gave a list of 39 language options. Tom pressed 16, the code for English and waited again.

'Your call is important to us,' said the new message. 'We are committed to providing you with an excellent service. We have satisfied our targets for each month in the last two years. Now, please listen carefully to the following message from one of our sponsoring partners.'

There was a faint click and then Tom heard a male voice. 'Medical emergencies are always difficult times,' said the man. The agency who had hired him had found an actor with a rich, warm voice. He sounded kindly and sympathetic. In the background Tom could hear comforting organ music being played. Although he recognised it as something by Bach he couldn't decide precisely what. 'At times like this we all feel frightened and anxious. But we often also feel angry and upset. We may feel that the emergency with which we are dealing could be the result of someone else's carelessness or incompetence. At times like this there is only one sensible action to take: to seek immediate expert help from someone who cares about you and your problem. Delay can be very damaging to your aims. We have many years of experience of dealing with problems of all kinds and we know that most people want to make sure that no one else is allowed to fall victim to the same error, the same carelessness or the same incompetence. To help satisfy this aim we provide a comprehensive legal service designed to defend your interests and to prosecute those responsible. And although we know that money can never be a cure for pain in the heart, we do our utmost to ensure that the pain and distress which have been caused are made a little lighter by the payment of the most substantial sum possible. To speak to one of our accredited and fully qualified experts press one, to continue with your call press two and to obtain full information about our other forms of legal representation press three.'

Tom pressed two and waited.

'Thank you for calling,' said a female voice which may or may not have been the original voice Tom had heard. 'Your call is important to us. All our operators are busy dealing with other emergencies at the moment but your call is in a queue and will be dealt with as soon as possible. Meanwhile, please keep holding and listen to the following messages from our partner sponsors.'

A man's voice then broke in. The first few words were cut by clumsy editing but it didn't matter much.

'... sad fact of life that despite the miracles so often worked by doctors, nurses, aides, laboratory technicians and others involved in professional health care, illness can often result in the demise of the one we love. At times like this we often feel confused, bewildered and worried. What must we do? How do we cope? What are our obligations? To whom can we turn? These are difficult questions at any time but when they occur in the aftermath of a sad personal loss they are doubly, trebly difficult to cope with. Our EUDCE approved funeral undertakers can help you thread your way through the dark and difficult days ahead. To obtain advice, a no-obligation quote and a chance to win a mobile telephone with three free historically significant ring tones simply press six. To continue holding press one.'

Tom pressed one.

'I'm afraid all our specialist operatives are still busy dealing with emergency calls,' said the female voice again, 'but you will soon be rising fast to the top of the queue and your call, which is important to us, will be dealt with very soon. Meanwhile, please listen to the following message from one of our partner sponsors.'

Tom sighed and waited.

'Organ donation and supply has come a long way in the last few years,' said a woman, who spoke with a slightly squeaky voice. She spoke very quickly, obviously anxious to get as much message as possible into the allotted time. 'Whether you are a would-be organ donor or a recipient-to-be it is our aim to help you speedily and with the least possible inconvenience. Our service is widely recognised to be the best in the world and is endorsed by a number of celebrities including Olympic Sudoku bronze medallist Voluptua Bottomley. Our supply service offers fully guaranteed livers, kidneys, hearts, eyes, lungs and other organs at the very lowest prices – ask now for details of our buy one get one free offer which must end soon – while our skilled and highly qualified purchasing team, working in our organ purchasing partner division offers the very best prices for previously owned organs. Whether you are selling an unwanted organ of your own, or an organ which belonged to a loved one, or you are selling a vital organ under our pre-deceasement cash-now scheme, you will be staggered by our keen prices. Don't sell your kidneys anywhere else until you've had a quote from us. Our surgeons, whether installing or removing, are among the best available and many are fully qualified. Our teams also provide full after care.'

There was a click as the message ended. Tom lowered the handset for a moment and looked at it as though he blamed it for the recordings he'd been listening to. Or, perhaps, as though he still found it difficult to believe that he'd heard what he'd been listening to. The kiosk was scarred where previous callers, driven to rage by waiting for the recordings to end, had attacked the receiver and the walls with the seemingly indestructible handset.

'Your call is important...' said the familiar female voice, coming back. But before she could continue she was interrupted by another female voice.

'I'm afraid your time is up. To continue your important call please insert more money.'

Tom stared at the telephone and cursed. He reached into his pocket. It was empty. He slammed down the telephone and hurried back to the house. For the first time in his life he missed the simple, good old days when telephone kiosks had taken ID cards and had been equipped with fingerprint scanners.

Chapter 9

'You bloody fool!' snarled Tschotchke, when Tom explained what had happened.

'How is he?'

Tchotchke looked down and kicked Perovskite with his foot. The Senior Inspector opened his eyes and looked up.

'Still alive – just' said Tschotchke, sounding disappointed. He handed Tom two coins. 'Hurry up!' he said. 'And don't come back without an ambulance.'

Tom headed back for the door.

'You're going to pay for this!' he snarled. 'I'm going to make sure that you, your aunt and your wife all die.'

'But they had nothing to do with it!' protested Tom.

'They're guilty by association,' said the sprout. 'They can be punished just as easily as you can.'

Tom knew that the sprout was right. Sprouts had enormous power over suspects. Any sprout could arrest a suspect and turn them over to the European Defence and Public Protection Regulatory Force. And suspects' families were often arrested under the 'guilty by association' laws which meant that a suspect who knew, or was closely related to, another suspect could be charged with the full offence.

Moreover, in the world controlled by EUDCE, suspects had no rights. The soulless and the ruthless bullied the helpless and the innocent with impunity. In a clever political move EUDCE commissioners had given all EUDCE suspects American citizenship. This had been promoted as a great achievement, a cause for much celebrating and another step towards world peace and eternal happiness for all. The fact that sprouts were not included in the deal had been widely regarded as a blow to EUDCE employees. It was announced that they had been excluded from this agreement because of their oath of loyalty to the European project. A small group of angry sprouts protested in public but the protests were half-hearted and quickly subsided. It was later suspected that these protests had been orchestrated by EUDCE itself

It was only weeks after the agreement had been signed that the reasoning behind it became apparent. Britain had previously signed an extradition agreement with the USA, enabling the Americans to extradite Britons who had broken American laws, and this treaty had later been expanded to cover the new United States of Europe. The combination of the two treaties meant that since every suspect in Europe was officially also an American citizen and, therefore, subject to American law, any suspect who broke the law in Europe would also be breaking the law in America and liable, therefore, to extradition. The agreement saved EUDCE the cost and trouble of providing lawyers, trials and prisons for suspects. ('The whole idea of having trials is a calculated insult to our security services,' one judge had famously announced. 'Arranging trials implies an unacceptable level of trust in the probity of security staff and, therefore, a lack of faith in the State itself. If the officers employed by the State say that someone is guilty then that should be enough for the State.')

All suspects who were arrested under this new arrangement (and who were not considered guilty of crimes meriting execution) were transported to one of the African or South American countries with which the USA had made arrangements. Once there, suspects would be held in a state of limbo. They were never tried or convicted and so, since they had never been sentenced, they could never appeal against their sentences.

To have a suspect arrested, charged, sentenced and deported a sprout simply had to fill in a form called a GB746 in which he detailed the suspect's crime against the State. Sprouts routinely picked out anyone who looked 16 years or older and seemed fairly fit. They drew the line at the frail and the sick. They didn't send small children. But they'd send 12-year-olds who looked 16. Either sex.

Once at their destination suspects were fitted with sternal implant tracker microchips to ensure that they did not escape (after some suspects had used pieces of razor blade to cut out subdermal implants, the authorities had taken to putting a microchip into each suspect's sternum, using a gun that looked and worked rather like a staple gun – it was an excruciatingly painful procedure and no anaesthetic was used). And then they were put to work in the fields.

The desperate need for crops (both for food and biofuel), and the shortage of oil for running farm equipment, meant that vast armies of labourers were needed. Land had to be prepared by hand. Seeds had to be sown by hand. Crops had to be harvested by hand. The global water shortage meant that crops had to be tended carefully, by hand, and watered individually to ensure that there was no waste.

Controlled and managed by Monsanto-Goldman-Sachs on behalf of EUDCE, huge areas of Africa had been planted with staple crops such as wheat, corn, soya and tobacco. (EUDCE still made huge amounts of money selling tobacco crops to addicted smokers around the world.) These crops needed constant attention. Designated European criminals (those who were suspected and, therefore, convicted of having committed crimes) were the perfect source of long-term labour and a vital replacement for the countless millions of indigent Africans who had died of starvation during the second decade of the 21st century when genetically engineered crops succumbed to a lethal virus and created a supranational famine which had, to no one's great surprise, impacted least of all on the USA and Europe and most of all on the developing world.

The imported workers lived in small, simple, wooden cabins. They worked half naked, dressed in the remains of the clothes in which they had arrived; they bathed, if they chose to do so, in a tin tub (in water that was changed once a week and which looked like mud within an hour) and they envied those among their number who had the foresight or the good luck to arrive wearing stout shoes or boots. Women who arrived wearing high heels and chose to walk barefoot rarely lasted more than a week. Cut feet turned septic within hours. Workers who fell ill and were unable to work were moved into a hut decorated with a EUDCE flag and a sign describing it as the local 'EUDCE Hospital' but there were no beds and no nurses, no doctors and no medicines. A study had shown that new workers were so cheaply 'recruited' that there was no financial benefit to be obtained by treating ones who fell sick. Patients (if that is the right word to describe people who are registered to receive medical treatment but not actually receiving any) lay, untreated, in the dark until they died. Every evening two workers would drag out the dead bodies and toss them onto an ever-burning bonfire so that their ashes could be used to fertilise the land. The stench of burning flesh covered the countryside for miles around.

Chapter 10

Tom, who was half way to the front door, ready to run back to the telephone point, stopped and turned back. He knew that the sprout spoke the truth. European law meant that close relatives and associates could be held legally responsible for the actions of those close to them. As in Communist Russia, just being related to a criminal (or, rather, someone accused of a crime against the State, the two not being the same thing in principle but being very much the same thing in practice) was every bit as bad as being a criminal. In that moment Tom made a decision that changed his life, and the lives of many others, for ever. It was a moment that was, much later, to be referred to as the very beginning of the beginning.

'What are you messing around for?' demanded the sprout. Tom noticed, for the first time, that in his lapel he wore a small bronze-coloured metal badge. The sprouts received these when they had sent 10 suspects to Africa. Send 20 and you were awarded a silver badge. Those who sent 50 wore a gold badge. The more ruthless sprouts sent everyone for whom they could complete a GB746. 'Get to the phone. Call an ambulance. And don't forget to tell them it's for an inspector or I'll make sure they shoot you twice.' He looked at Tom and laughed. 'If I tell the police you pushed him, his dependants, if he's got any, will receive double compensation and an enhanced pension.'

Tom stood still for a moment then moved past the standing sprout and headed for the kitchen.

'Now, where the hell are you going?'

'It's quicker this way. I can cut through the back.'

The sprout considered this for a moment and then nodded. In the kitchen Tom's aunt was sitting at the table staring into space. She did this quite a lot, sometimes sitting quite still for hours at a time. At other times she didn't seem able to stop moving. It was impossible to know how she was going to be on any particular day. She turned as her nephew entered the room.

'Hello!' whispered Tom.

'Hello,' his aunt whispered back. She smiled at him. She was sitting in a front seat from a BMW which had been placed beside the stove in the kitchen. She had her cat, Tabatha, on her lap. The cat, nearly 20-years-old, was the centre of her universe. For a moment it looked as though she might have recognised Tom but then she began to look puzzled. 'Have you seen my nephew?' she asked. Again, she whispered because he had done.

'He's around,' Tom said softly. He no longer tried to correct her, or reason with her too much. She quickly became upset if she realised that she was getting things wrong.

'Do you want a cup of tea?' she asked.

'I'll make one,' he said. 'In a minute. I've got something else to do first.'

Chapter 11

Afterwards, Tom examined the frying pan. There was no sign that it had been used for anything other than frying eggs. He put it in the sink. He thought it needed a wash. He then filled a small kettle with water and placed it on a hook over their small kitchen fire.

'Would you like a biscuit with your tea?' asked his aunt. This was, he knew, her gentle way of saying that she would.

He opened a cupboard and took out a packet of ginger biscuits. They were soft and well past their best-before date but they still looked and almost tasted like biscuits. He took two biscuits out of the packet, put them on a cracked saucer and put them in front of his aunt. She smiled, said thank you, picked one up and started to nibble at it. She nibbled like a bird. Like everyone else she ate slowly to get the most out of the experience. She could make a single biscuit last a quarter of an hour.

'We can't have bodies at the bottom of the stairs,' complained his aunt, between nibbles. 'We will have to move them. We can't be clambering over bodies every time we want to go somewhere. Someone might trip up.'

Tom sat down opposite his aunt. He felt very, very tired. He realised suddenly that while the advantage of being older is that people don't expect you do unexpected things (like hitting them on the head with frying pans) the disadvantage is that you get tired after doing those things.

'Aren't you having a biscuit?' his aunt asked.

'Not just now, thanks,' Tom replied. 'I'm not hungry at the moment.' When he told her that he wasn't hungry it wasn't usually true. This time it was true. He didn't have the energy to eat.

He looked at his aunt and realised that she was seemingly unconcerned by her efforts. And she was twenty years older than him. That made him feel even older.

Chapter 12

Half an hour later, when his wife came home, Tom still hadn't moved. He was sitting at the kitchen table, with his hands cupped around a now cold cup of tea. His aunt had nearly finished her second biscuit. He heard Dorothy's key in the front door, and then heard her gasp with shock or surprise as she walked down the hallway.

Dorothy, Tom's wife, was 54. She had been a successful sculptor whose work had been bought by many discerning collectors. She was tall, just four inches shorter than Tom, and looked ten years younger than she was. Her eyes were deep brown and her skin still china white. The whiteness of her skin embarrassed her a little because she thought it drew attention to the greyness of her pitted teeth. Because of this she rarely showed her teeth when she smiled and people who didn't know her thought of her as being rather aloof. She sometimes envied those who wore false teeth. Dentures weren't affected by the fluoride in the drinking water.

Most female suspects dressed like car mechanics or plasterers and, as a result, looked just about as attractive. Dorothy, however, still made an effort. She did this not for Tom, who would have loved her in baggy hessian trousers and a canvas poncho, but for herself 'If I dress like everyone else,' she said once, 'I might well forget who I am. Worse, I might think like everyone else too.'

The demand for works of art had more or less disappeared under the authority of a fascist bureaucracy which regarded a blue flag studded with gold stars as the height of artistic perfection and so Dorothy worked unofficially and illegally as a private messenger, carrying letters and packets around the area. The Post Office had been replaced by a EUDCE approved mail distributor based in Turin. (Deliveries had been cut to once a week on the grounds that more frequent deliveries were both unnecessary and a danger to the environment). There was, therefore, a great demand for her services.

'I suppose you already know this,' said Dorothy, walking into the kitchen. 'But I had to step over two people lying down in the halfway. They seem to be asleep.' She was, he knew, calmer than he would have been if their roles had been reversed. 'Or, possibly, dead.'

'Sprouts,' said Tom. He reached out and took her hands. They loved each other very much, and had done so for a long time. 'Both of them. They came to inspect our labels.'

'Are they dead?'

Tom nodded.

'What happened?'

'One fell down the stairs. The other one I hit on the head with a frying pan.' Tom thought about it for a moment. 'Actually,' he said, 'I think my aunt did most of the damage.'

'With the frying pan?'

'Yes.'

'And they're both dead.'

'They seem pretty dead to me. I wouldn't sell them life insurance.'

'That's all right then,' said Dorothy.

'One fell down the stairs. I killed the other one, the second one, because he was going to claim that I killed the first one. Do you want some tea?'

'But you didn't kill the first one?'

'No, no. Well, a bit. Sort of. The small fat one just tripped and fell. But they'd have believed the other one rather than me. So I had to kill the second one. And then finish off the first one.'

'Of course they would,' agreed Dorothy, nodding.

'He was threatening to have us all arrested, charged, imprisoned and all the rest of it.'

Dorothy shivered. 'Two down and a lot left to go.'

Tom looked at her.

'There are a lot of sprouts in EUDCE, aren't there?'

Tom nodded.

'So it's two down and a lot to go.'

'You don't mind?'

'About you killing sprouts?'

'Yes.'

'No, why should I mind. I don't mind at all. I expect they had it coming. Incidentally, one of them has what looks like one of my bras poking out of his jacket pocket. I recognise it because it's faded pink and has a mended strap.'

'They both do.'

'Do what?'

'Have one of your bras in their jacket pockets.'

'Oh.' She raised an eyebrow. 'Right. I won't ask. You've clearly had a busy afternoon.'

'The bras both had imperial measurements on the labels. But you can have the bras back now that they're dead.'

'Oh good. That's a relief Have you any idea how difficult it is to find underwear these days? Even if I had money to spend on bras I don't know where I'd find any for sale. I'm glad we'll get those back. My breasts will be pleased.' She looked down at her chest, as though expecting some sign of delight.

'The strange thing is that I don't feel in the slightest bit bad about it,' said Tom. He paused and thought for a moment. 'An hour or two ago if you'd asked me if I could kill someone I would have laughed at you and said 'No! Never. Not under any circumstances.' But now that I've done it I don't feel bad about it at all.' He bit his lip and thought for a moment or two. 'Perhaps because I just didn't think of them as people.' He paused again. 'If I ran over a dog or a cat by accident I'd feel really bad about it. But I don't feel bad about those two in the hall.'

Dorothy reached out and touched Tom's hand.

He put his other hand on top of her hand. For a moment they just sat and looked each other. 'I know we'll have to do something with them, but can I get you some tea now?'

'I'd love some.' She smiled. 'You really are very English, you know.'

'Am I?'

'There are two bodies in the hall and you're making a cup of tea.'

'You said you'd like a cup.'

She shrugged. 'So, I'm very English too.'

'Maybe a cup of tea will help us decide what to do?'

'Let's hope so. Incidentally, what did you say you used to kill the one that you killed?'

'A frying pan.'

'Ah. Surprising choice. But doubtless effective.'

'The whole thing sort of happened,' he explained. Tom turned to his aunt who was still sitting at the kitchen table. 'Would you like another cup of tea?'

Tom's aunt looked up.

'Another cup of tea?' Tom held up his cup.

She smiled and nodded. 'And a biscuit?'

Suddenly, the Telescreen burst into life as a breeze started to turn the community windmill. A plump, middle-aged woman was sitting on a large red chair answering questions from a small man with a neat moustache and a wig. The moustache looked as if it might well have been false too. The woman had blue lips and was wheezing. She didn't look well.

'What's this?' asked Tom.

'It's a new programme,' explained Dorothy. 'Contestants answer questions and if they do well they can win an operation. The operation is then done live on the Telescreen the following day. And the gloriously happy patients get to spend up to a week recovering in a sprout hospital afterwards.'

'A week? They get to spend a week in the hospital?' This was unheard of. EUDCE's Care in the Community scheme had been expanded to include hospital patients, who, if they were lucky enough to have an operation, were invariably sent home to be cared for by their families and friends within hours of leaving the operating theatre. To the embarrassment of some senior clinicians evidence showed that patients who were cared for at home were less likely to die than patients who were cared for in hospital. There was far less risk of contracting a deadly infection at home. And fewer recovering patients died of starvation. Hospital infections had become endemic and at least half of all hospital patients died from them.

'Is it compulsory? The hospital stay?'

'No, no, I don't think so. I think it's rather regarded as a perk. Something that no one in their right mind would even contemplate turning down.'

'And contestants can win big operations?'

'Oh yes. Heart surgery, brain surgery, bowel resections, breast enlargement, hip replacements – all sorts of stuff.' This was quite a prize. Operations of any size were not usually available to suspects, although it was possible for suspects to win some surgical operations and medical treatments if they bought a winning ticket for the European Lottery.

'Do the winners get to choose what operation they have done?'

Dorothy shook her head and smiled. 'Oh, no. They get what they win. A woman last week won a penis enlargement operation. She was hoping for an operation to remove a lump in her lung. She burst into tears when they told her what she'd won. She was dying of cancer. It was very sad. She's in the lead to win a trolley full of groceries for crying louder and longer than anyone else on the Telescreen this month.'

'Your final question,' said the small quizmaster, a man called Milksop, who had initially won fame and popularity among EUDCE bureaucrats for his skill in asking apparently caustic, tough questions which, in reality, allowed his interviewees to wriggle off the hook without anyone noticing, and who was now capitalising on his two dimensional fame by hosting a series of bland quiz programmes. He wore a purple satin suit and a blond wig with pink highlights. 'Answer this one correctly and you will win today's surprise operation.' He paused, as quizmasters always do, in order to build up the drama and to enable the studio director to catch a shot of the contestant's face as the agony tension built up.

'Does the woman who won the trolley full of stuff get to choose her own groceries?' asked Tom, quietly, during the pause.

Dorothy shook her head. 'She just gets what they give her. It's usually bulky stuff that doesn't cost too much. They put a few fancy things on the top, packets of biscuits, toothpaste and so on, but underneath it's mainly toilet rolls and cat litter, that sort of stuff.'

'What if you don't have a cat?'

Dorothy looked at him.

The quizmaster studied the card he was holding. 'At the end of this week's Global G3 meeting in Miami, held to end world poverty and hunger, the delegates from the United States of Europe, China and the United States of America enjoyed a formal dinner together. How many courses were there?'

The contestant closed her eyes as she thought about the answer.

'Fourteen?' she suggested, rather fearfully, after a few moments.

Again, the host made her wait. The camera zoomed in on the contestant's face which was now as grey as her teeth. She seemed terrified, like an animal caught in a car's headlights.

'Why do they do this?' asked Tom. 'Make people wait so long to know if they've won.'

'To build up the tension, I suppose,' said Dorothy.

'If they build up much more tension she is definitely going to die,' said Tom firmly.

'Correeeeeeeeect!' cried Milksop eventually, throwing his arms in the air and feigning excitement but somehow doing so without much conviction or success. He was not a good actor. He beamed at the contestant who really did look quite ill. Even the knowledge that she had won didn't seem to improve her appearance.

'If they don't hurry this up she's going to die in the studio,' said Tom.

'And now let's find out what you've won...,' The host took a small envelope from his inside jacket pocket and once again the woman had to wait. Milksop opened the envelope, which was not sealed, and took from it a small slip of paper, folded once.

'I bet they reuse that envelope time and time again,' said Tom.

Dorothy laughed.

'You're going to love this!' cried the host, having read what was on the paper. He turned to the woman and put an arm around her.

'You've won...'

He waited.

She tried to look at the paper to see what was written there but he held it away from her.

'You've won breast enlargement surgery!' he cried at last. 'Both breasts!' he added, as though contestants were sometimes offered one-sided enhancement surgery.

The woman, who already had vast breasts and who would, if anything, have probably preferred a breast reduction operation, looked terribly disappointed.

'Poor thing,' said Dorothy. 'She must be a 44F already. It's probably the last thing she wants.'

'How the hell is the surgeon going to make them bigger?' asked Tom, not unreasonably.

'Are you excited?' asked Milksop.

The woman was trying hard to look brave.

'Oh, yes,' she lied without any conviction.

'Just what you've always wanted?'

The woman nodded. A first tear trickled down her left cheek. 'Well, I was really hoping for a heart operation,' she admitted, wheezily. 'But you have to take what you can get don't you?'

'Another brave and lucky winner here on *Win Your Dream Operation!*' cried the host. 'Tune in tomorrow at the same time to see our next contestant. And don't forget to tune in at ten to see today's lucky winner having her operation – live on your BBC!'

The screen changed to a shot of an audience clapping wildly. The programme wasn't really filmed in front of an audience. The programme makers just used standard film of an enthusiastic audience clapping and cheering. The audience members, all suspects, had been given a loaf of bread each to cheer and shout excitedly for an hour.

'What's on now?' asked Tom.

Dorothy pressed a button on the screen so that they could access the programme selection.

'You can choose between *Cannibal Island* and *Thongs of Praise*,' said Dorothy.

'I'm no wiser.'

'*Cannibal Island* is billed as the ultimate reality programme. A dozen suspects are marooned on an island with nothing to eat. The winner is the person who's left at the end of twelve weeks.'

Tom shuddered. 'And *Thongs of Praise*?'

'It's promoted as 'a religious programme with a difference'. The congregation all wear skimpy panties.'

'Maybe we can just sit and watch the fire,' suggested Tom. 'While we decide what to do with the bodies in the hall.'

'Sounds good to me,' agreed Dorothy.

Tom's aunt, who had said nothing for a while, smiled and nodded at them both and took advantage of the quiet to ask if anyone wanted another biscuit.

Chapter 13

One cup of tea each, and twenty seven minutes later, they had what they both agreed would turn out to be either an excellent, well thought out plan or, heaven forbid, a disastrous, mess of a scheme.

It had been Dorothy's idea.

'The best place to hide something is often in the most obvious place of all,' she said. 'Where's the one place that people are most likely to die?'

'Dunno,' said Tom. He thought for a while. 'In a cemetery?'

'They don't die there.'

'On the roads? Dump the two of them in a gutter in the hope that whoever finds them will think they were hit and run victims?'

Dorothy thought for a moment. 'Not a bad idea,' she admitted. 'But I think my idea is better.'

'Go on then, where?'

'In the hospital.'

Tom stared at her and frowned.

'People are always dying in hospitals,' she pointed out. 'No one will take too much notice of a couple of extra bodies. If we could put the bodies in empty beds the staff will assume they died there.'

Dorothy had, since childhood, been a diabetic. She had, over the years, been a frequent visitor to the hospital. Like many long- term patients she knew how the local hospital worked as well as, or better than, most of the staff. She'd seen the hospital grow and she'd seen it decline.

'Don't they, sort of, keep count of the patients?'

'The admissions system is all computerised,' Dorothy pointed out.

'I know how to access the computer. Do you know their names?'

'I can find them.'

They went back into the hall. The two bodies had begun to stiffen. Tom rescued Dorothy's bras and handed them to her, and then removed the incriminating notebook from the fat sprout's pocket. He took out their plastic identification wallets. Dorothy took the bras from him as though they were contaminated and then put them on the stairs. 'I think I'll wash these before I wear them again,' she said. Tom put the sprout's notebook on the fire in the kitchen. He also burned the identification papers he had taken from the two men. The notebook was half empty and for a moment Tom was tempted to tear out the used pages and keep the rest. It was a long time since he'd had the luxury of a notebook to put in his pocket. But he knew that would have been a dangerous thing to do. Helped by Tom's aunt, who was much stronger than she looked, and who didn't seem in the slightest bit surprised that they were now dragging bodies through the house, Dorothy and Tom half carried and half dragged the two sprouts through the kitchen, out of the back door and into the small yard at the back of the house where Tom kept his bicycle and, more importantly, the small wooden trailer which he used for carrying logs and vegetables back to the house. Occasionally, Tom used the trailer to help Dorothy with bigger deliveries in the neighbourhood.

'It'll be a squeeze to get them both in at once,' said Dorothy.

'We have to,' replied Tom. 'I don't want to have to make two trips.'

Tom removed the back of the trailer and he and Dorothy crammed in the larger of the two corpses. They then lay the smaller corpse on top of it. The legs of the biggest corpse stuck out. They didn't have an old carpet in which to wrap the bodies ('How come people in films always have a spare carpet handy?' asked Tom) so they covered them first with an old blanket, then an old sheet, next with some sheets of cardboard and finally with a sheet of rusting corrugated iron which they took off the roof of their small shed. They used an old washing line to tie the load onto the trailer. The result was a mess but it had the dubious advantage of looking so untidy that it didn't look as if they were trying to hide something. It looked as if they were wheeling rubbish to a recycling centre.

'It looks terribly heavy,' said Dorothy.

Tom hitched the trailer to the tow bar on his bicycle, climbed onto the bicycle and pressed down on the pedal. It took all his effort but he managed to move forwards a foot or two. 'It'll be all right once I've got moving,' he said. 'Just keep your fingers crossed that I don't have to stop suddenly.'

And then they waited for it to get dark.

Tom put water in the saucepan he hadn't used to kill the sprout and put the pan on the stove. As the water first boiled he added a few potatoes, a couple of carrots, a swede and finally some stale bread that was too hard to eat.

By the time the three of them had finished eating the resultant stew, it was dark. They stacked the dirty dishes in the sink and treated themselves to a rare coffee. Tea was difficult to find, and expensive, but coffee was usually available only on the black market. A man who regularly employed Dorothy to deliver messages had a supply of instant coffee and occasionally gave her a jar as a tip. The jars were always long past their 'Best Before' date but neither Tom nor Dorothy cared about that.

'Is it too soon?' asked Dorothy, when she and Tom had both finished their coffee. They had made the drinks last as long as humanly possible in order to give themselves something to do while they waited. Those who talk about bravery and courage often forget that it is only the fearful who can be truly brave. The stupid, the thoughtless, the unimaginative, the reckless and the impulsive may appear to be brave but often their actions are merely a result of their failure to understand the consequences of what they are doing. And the real courage must be found by those who must wait; enduring those eternal minutes of fearful expectation without giving up or abandoning their plans.

Tom looked at the old clock on the wall.

'What are we going to do with your aunt?' asked Dorothy, nodding in the direction of Tom's aunt, who was nibbling another biscuit, her fifth of the day.

'Do you think we can leave her here?'

Dorothy looked at him, looked at his aunt, thought for a moment and then shook her head. 'No. She might wander off.' His aunt's dementia was still in the early stages and she had moments of lucidity but on several occasions Tom had had to comb the streets looking for her. One early evening he'd found her in a local park. She'd been standing next to a lake, crying. Very few people walked in parks, especially after dusk. Anyone who did so could be arrested under the For Your Own Safety Curfew.

He touched his aunt gently on her shoulder. 'Get your coat,' he said. 'We're going out.' His aunt smiled with delight. She rushed to the back door, grabbed her coat off the hook and put it on. She then picked up the cat and held it, unprotesting, in her arms.

'You can't take the cat!' said Tom.

His aunt's response was to cling ever tighter to the cat. Feeling squeezed, and unable to breathe, Tabatha started to struggle.

'OK,' said Tom softly. 'Bring the cat. But don't squeeze it too tight. And for heavens sake don't let it wander off.' His aunt kissed the cat on the nose and relaxed her grip. The cat stopped struggling.

And then they set off. Tom riding the bicycle. The two dead sprouts in the trailer. And Dorothy and Tom's aunt (with the cat) walking behind.

Chapter 14

Apart from one scary moment when the trailer nearly tipped over, spilling its contents on the road, the journey to the hospital went more smoothly than they could have hoped. Tom rode his bicycle and towed the trailer with the two corpses in it. The added weight of the trailer meant that he couldn't have travelled at much above walking pace even if he'd wanted to. Dorothy and Tom's aunt (at Tom's insistence, carrying Tabatha in a shopping bag) walked along the pavement. Occasionally, Tom slowed a little to allow the two women to catch up with him. Dorothy kept an eye on the trailer to make sure that the cargo didn't slip. The streets at that time of night were dark and almost deserted. There were no revellers, and no drinkers wobbling home, because there were no pubs. The public houses that had survived the ban on smoking had eventually succumbed when the ban on drinking alcohol in public places had been introduced. These days people sat at home and drank and smoked alone. Naturally, to help ease their loneliness, they drank and smoked far more than they had ever smoked and drunk when they'd been able to do so in company.

The energy crisis meant that there were no street lights. The roads were pitch black. The lack of light, and the lack of people in the streets, meant that there were no CCTV cameras switched on. The cameras (the ones that hadn't been stolen) were still there (most thieves had quickly realised that there was no point in stealing things for which there was no market). But they weren't switched on. There wasn't enough electricity to run them and EUDCE didn't have the money to spend on hiring people to watch the pictures they took.

The only people out and about were shadowy householders dumping rubbish in the gutters and shadowy scavengers searching through what had been thrown away in the hope that they could find something to eat or to wear or to sell. Dumping rubbish was illegal but everyone did it. The official recycling centres were miles away. Tom knew two men who had been caught, charged, arrested and deported for breaking into people's homes and dumping rubbish in them. And he knew a former surveyor who spent his nights searching for empty food tins. The man earned pennies for food by peeling off the labels and selling them to a man who turned them into pulp from which he made hand-made paper. Occasionally, a few suspects would hold a dog roast in the street but these were frowned on by the sprouts because people seemed to enjoy them.

The only motorised traffic belonged to sprouts, travelling on official business (or on business they said was official, which wasn't necessarily the same thing at all). Suspects had no cars. Only sprouts had access to what little oil was left.

At the hospital Tom parked his bicycle in a dark corner of the almost empty car park.

'Wait here,' said Dorothy. 'I'll get a trolley.'

Tom looked at her.

'We can't just carry the bodies into the hospital,' she explained.

'But no one will look at us if we're wheeling a body in on a trolley.'

It was ten minutes before she returned, pushing a hospital trolley. Lying on top of the trolley were a white sheet, a red blanket and a white coat.

'Put on the coat,' she told Tom. 'I borrowed it from the staff room.'

'Did anyone see you?'

'No. It was deserted.'

Tom put on the coat. And then, after untying the rope holding the bodies in the trailer, he and Dorothy manoeuvred the top corpse up onto the trolley. It was much more difficult than they thought it would be. Tom found himself cursing the body he was struggling to manhandle. But, as he started to get angry, he remembered that if he got angry he would become impatient and that if he became impatient he would be careless. And carelessness would lead direct to death. For the three of them. He took deep breaths and calmed down. Once he'd managed to heave the body onto the trolley he and Dorothy then covered it with the sheet and the blanket.

'You push the trolley,' said Dorothy. 'Your aunt and I will walk along beside as though we're worried relatives.'

And that's exactly what they did.

No one spared them a glance.

The hospital accident department looked like an Arabian indoor market. Suspects weren't usually entitled to be admitted to hospital for care. Their only hope of seeing a doctor was to sit and wait and hope that they would one day be seen. If there was a queue it was difficult to see where it started and where it ended. In a corner three men were brewing tea on a small fire. No one seemed to have noticed. If they had noticed they didn't care. Only sprouts were admitted for medium or long-term treatment.

'Where do we go now?' asked Tom, when they'd passed through the accident and emergency unit. Despite the time of night the unit was remarkably busy. A drunk was arguing loudly with a nurse. He was twice her size and attempting to be threatening, but she looked bored and unconcerned and not in the slightest bit frightened. A man and a woman, both white-faced, were sitting holding hands, giving each other comfort. Tom felt more nervous now. He could feel his shirt sticking to his back. When he'd been riding the bicycle, and pulling the trailer, he'd had to work hard and concentrate on where he was going. He hadn't had time to worry. Now the worries were piling up. What if someone found the body they'd left out in the car park? He'd left it in the trailer, covered with the cardboard, the old sheet and the corrugated iron. But what if someone tried to steal the bicycle. Damn! He should have at least locked the bicycle. He looked around. Everyone seemed busy with their own problems but how long would it be before someone asked him who he was, why he was wearing a white coat and why he was pushing a patient along the corridor.

'Down the corridor straight ahead,' replied Dorothy. 'Just keep going down the main corridor.' She sounded calm and that helped Tom.

'This is the hospital,' said Tom's aunt suddenly.

'Yes,' agreed Tom.

'Is someone poorly?'

'No, we're just visiting,' said Tom.

'Go right,' said Dorothy suddenly.

Tom turned the trolley into another corridor. It was darker and the walls were lined with empty trolleys.

'Just stop here a moment.'

'Where are we taking him?'

'I was thinking of putting him into a bed,' said Dorothy. 'But this is much better. Less chance of being noticed, or getting caught.'

'Here?' asked Tom in surprise.

'This corridor leads down to the scanner. They don't use this much at night. We can leave him here.'

Tom looked at her.

'Where?'

'Just park the trolley,' she said. She moved an empty trolley out of the way so that there was a space. 'Put the trolley there and we'll use this empty trolley to fetch the other body. It makes more sense for two patients to have been forgotten down here, and to be together, than for two patients to be forgotten in different parts of the hospital,' said Dorothy.

'What happens when they find them?' asked Tom.

'They'll think they were admitted and then forgotten,' said Dorothy.

'But would they have got this far without going through the official admissions system?'

'Probably not,' agreed Dorothy. 'But I'll put them into the computer. It will look as though they were admitted and then just lost and forgotten. The porters are always losing patients. They park a patient somewhere, go off for a fag and then forget about it.'

Dorothy led Tom and Tom's aunt (still carrying the bag containing the cat) back into the main corridor and then down another corridor.

'Where does this go?'

'The women's medical ward,' whispered Dorothy. 'They don't admit new patients here at night because they have a special admissions ward. I just want the computer in the ward manager's office.' She opened a door into a small room which contained a desk, a chair and a computer. Everything in the room was old and looked tired and well past its best. A noticeboard fixed to the wall was thick with papers fastened to it with coloured pins.

It was a real squeeze for the three of them (and the cat) to get into the room so that they could close the door and turn on the light.

'How are you going to access the computer?' asked Tom. 'Don't they have passwords and stuff?'

'Of course,' said Dorothy. 'But look!' She pointed to the computer. It was, like most of the ones in use, an old-fashioned one with a cracked and dirty case. A small red light signified that, against the rules, it had been left on stand-by and at the top of the screen, in the flat area above the screen, a sticky label, curling at one corner where the gum had come partly unstuck, gave the ward manager's undoubtedly useful aide memoire. Her access code, ultra secret password and personal identity number had been neatly written on the small label.

('How does anyone expect us to remember all this stuff?' the ward manager had demanded when a colleague had remonstrated with her. 'I've got different four digit pin numbers for my bank card and for three credit cards. I've got a password to access my e-mail address and a code word I have to give when I telephone the bank. The lock on my bicycle can only be opened by putting in the correct four digit code and to get into my flat I need another four digit code. I've got passwords and code numbers corning out of my ears. If anyone thinks I'm going to remember this lot as well then they've got another think corning.')

Dorothy typed in the access codes and Tom gave her the names of the two men. She put them into the system, both admitted as road accident victims.

'Switch on that printer would you,' she said.

'What on earth do you want a printer for?'

'I'll print out a couple of name labels. We'll label their wrists.'

'So that it looks as though they were officially admitted?'

Dorothy nodded.

When she had finished Dorothy closed down the computer, leaving it on standby. They turned off the light, closed the office door and headed back to where they'd left the body they'd brought into the hospital. Dorothy fastened the appropriate label to the wrist of the cadaver. They then headed back to where they'd left the other body.

To Tom's great relief the second body was where they'd left it. They loaded it onto the trolley in the same way as before. Dorothy fitted the label around the man's wrist and then Tom pushed the trolley through the hospital. Dorothy walked alongside and Tom's aunt, carrying the cat in her shopping bag, walked behind them. They had passed through the accident and emergency unit and were hurrying down the main corridor when they heard firm footsteps, half running, half walking, behind them. A man shouted.

'Excuse me! Could you stop a moment please?'

Tom and Dorothy both turned. The man following them down the corridor was short, round and red-faced. He had tiny eyes, puffy eyelids and a red flush on both cheeks. He looked to be in his sixties but might have been younger. He wore an ill-fitting uniform, complete with well-shined boots and a peaked cap, and was out of breath. Tom and Dorothy looked at each other and both stopped. They didn't speak. They didn't need to. There was nothing to be said.

'Sorry to bother you,' said the man, when he caught up with them. He was carrying a clipboard in his right hand and with his left hand he fiddled with his collar which seemed to be too tight. He had a small orange button fixed to the bottom of his left earlobe to show that although he was in uniform he was a contract employee, a 'trusty' and not a fully-registered EUDCE functionary. He looked at what was obviously a body, lying on the trolley and underneath the sheet, and then looked away as though it made him nervous.

'What's the problem?' asked Tom, trying to sound more confident than he felt.

'I didn't fill in your security clearance form,' said the security guard. He had bald patches and a tic near his left eye. They were symptoms Tom had seen many times among sprouts. They were, he knew, side effects associated with the drug treatment of Attention Deficit Hyperactivity Disorder (ADHD). Over 50% of both sprout and suspect populations had been officially diagnosed as suffering from ADHD. Among some populations within the United States of Europe, the figure was as high as 90%. A similar number had been diagnosed as autistic with the result that a large percentage of the population had been officially diagnosed as suffering from both. Children who had not been diagnosed as having one of these diseases were officially labelled 'nonpsychohyperresponsive' and regarded as inferior. Only sprouts and trustys received regular drug treatment.

The guard waved the clipboard around behind him. 'At the entrance. When you came into the hospital.' He looked embarrassed. 'I was on a comfort break,' he explained. 'Bit of prostate trouble, they say.' Trustys, like suspects, weren't entitled to comprehensive medical care. The guard would have to live with his prostate symptoms. If they became too troublesome, and interfered with his ability to do his job, he would be 'retired' without compensation or a pension.

'Ah,' nodded Tom, understanding.

'One of the receptionists told me,' explained the guard. 'Said she'd seen someone come in.'

'What do you need to know?' asked Tom.

The guard lifted his clipboard and removed a stub of pencil from his breast pocket.

'Still not used to these,' he said, holding up the pencil.

'You still miss the hand-held computer things?'

'Oh yes,' nodded the man. 'And heaven knows what happens to these.' He tapped the form with the pencil stub. 'I hand them in at the end of my shift and someone files them away.'

'Difficult times,' agreed Tom.

The guard sighed. 'Better get it over with then,' he said. 'Can you tell me what's on the trolley, please?'

'A body.'

'Human or other?'

'Oh, human.'

'EUDCE employee or suspect?'

'EUDCE employee.'

'Male or female?'

'Male.'

'Live or deceased?'

'Deceased.'

'Cause of death, if known?'

'Hit on the head several times with a frying pan.'

Tom, Dorothy and the guard all turned.

'We hit him on the head several times with a frying pan,' repeated Tom's aunt. She stared at them all, unblinkingly.

'Aha,' said the security guard. A small smile broke across his chubby features. 'A joke,' he said, flatly, letting it be known that he understood. Jokes weren't common.

'A joke,' agreed Tom.

The guard nodded. 'Shall I put 'unknown'?'

'That would be fine,' agreed Tom quickly. 'My aunt has an old-fashioned sense of humour.'

The guard wrote on his pad and then leant inches closer to Tom. 'Not always appreciated these days,' he murmured. 'Humour,' he explained, in case there was any doubt. He pulled at his shirt collar again. 'If you don't mind my mentioning it.'

'Absolutely,' Tom murmured back, nodding to show that he understood and agreed. 'My aunt is rather old,' he added as a sort of explanation. He could feel the sweat pouring down his back and his forehead. A drop of sweat fell off an eyebrow, landed on his cheek and ran down his face. He hoped the dim lighting would help ensure that the guard didn't see how nervous he was.

'Your relationships to the deceased?' The guard asked; he looked at the three of them. 'Relatives? Friends? Colleagues?'

'Colleagues,' said Tom.

The guard, who wanted to get back up the corridor so that he was nearer to the toilets, ticked the appropriate box on the form. 'That seems to be it, thank you very much, sir,' he said. He nodded to each of them in turn and started to walk away, back up the corridor towards the accident and emergency department. Tom had taken his place behind the trolley, ready to start pushing again, and the guard had travelled about five paces up the corridor, when the cat miaowed.

Tom, Dorothy and Tom's aunt froze. The guard turned.

'Was that a cat? Did I hear a cat?' demanded the guard. Suddenly, he didn't seem quite so polite. Suddenly, there was an edge in his voice. This, Tom and Dorothy sensed, was serious.

'It's my aunt's cat,' said Tom softly. He didn't think he could take much more tension. He feared that if he lost any more sweat they might all drown.

'In the bag?' asked the guard,

'In the bag,' agreed Tom. Gently, he took the bag from his aunt's hands and opened it. The cat, now settled at the bottom of the bag, looked up at them anxiously.

'Cats aren't allowed in the hospital,' said the guard firmly. 'No cats.'

'I'm sorry about that,' said Tom. 'My aunt doesn't like to leave it by itself. She worries.'

'There's been a lot of catnapping in our area,' said Dorothy.

'I've heard they make good eating,' said the guard. 'Bit like chicken.'

'I believe so,' said Tom.

'I have to ask you to remove the cat from the hospital,' said the guard.

'I'll take aunt outside,' said Dorothy softly. 'With the cat,' she added.

The guard nodded his approval.

'Thanks,' said Tom. He smiled nervously at the guard. The guard nodded; it was a sharp, rather abrupt nod.

Escorted by the guard, Dorothy, Tom's aunt and the cat headed back towards the hospital entrance. Tom, now alone, pushed the trolley back to the corridor leading down to the scanner, parked it and then walked back out of the hospital.

'I think we got away with it,' said Dorothy as they made their way back home.

'I think we did,' agreed Tom. He was riding the bicycle very slowly in the gutter. Dorothy and his aunt were walking along the pavement beside him.

'The man was very nice,' said Tom's aunt. 'He didn't seem to mind that we'd killed that chap with our frying pan.'

Tom and Dorothy looked at each other. 'No,' said Tom. 'That was nice of him.'

Chapter 15

Tom really didn't mean to kill the man from the Telescreen licensing people but he was, he discovered, surprisingly calm about it afterwards. He was so calm that when someone banged on the front door a few moments later he broke the habit of a lifetime and opened it. He was still holding the frying pan, as though he had been interrupted in some culinary activity when he had heard the knock.

'I'm from Telescreen licensing,' said a grey-faced man at the door, holding up a piece of plastic with his photograph on it. He smelt of luxury. Aftershave, talcum powder, hair gel and a freshly laundered shirt.

Tom stared at him.

'My colleague should be here,' explained the caller. 'I had some difficulty parking the van.'

'Of course,' said Tom. He stood aside to allow the caller room to enter and then closed the door. Then he raised the frying pan and brought it crashing down onto the back of the sprout's head.

Then he woke up.

When Dorothy woke she found that she was alone in bed. She got up, put on a slightly frayed Paisley dressing gown, and went downstairs. Tom was in the kitchen sipping a mug of tea.

'Have you been up long?'

Tom looked at the clock. 'Twenty, twenty five, minutes.' He pointed at his tea. 'Do you want a cup?'

Dorothy nodded. Tom made her one.

'I can't believe what we did yesterday,' said Tom when they were both sitting down. He spoke quietly as though nervous that someone might hear him.

'Do you think we got away with it?'

Tom nodded. 'I think so.' He sipped at his tea. 'I killed someone,' he said, as much to himself as to Dorothy. 'I would never have thought myself capable. I killed two people. He stopped and thought for a moment. 'Actually, I'm not sure I did kill either of them. My aunt seemed much better with the frying pan than I was.' He stared pensively at a stain on the table. 'She was very good at it,' he said. 'Ruthless. Utterly ruthless.' He shuddered involuntarily. It wasn't easy to reconcile the gentle, rather jolly aunt he thought he knew with the frying-pan wielding madwoman he had watched battering a man's head so efficiently. 'So I don't really know whether I killed one, two or none.'

'You didn't have any choice.'

'I know. But it seems strange. Part of me feels that I should feel guilty. But I'm not sure whether I do.' He sipped at his tea. 'In fact I'm pretty sure I don't.' He paused and thought. 'I don't.' He took another sip. 'And so I'm not sure whether I should feel guilty about not feeling guilty.'

'It doesn't count,' said Dorothy. 'They were sprouts.'

'I know it's wrong to kill people. But what else could I have done? You can't argue with sprouts. You can't discuss anything with them. You can't reason with them. They'd have arrested the three of us and handed us over to the Americans.'

'It's like a war,' said Dorothy. 'We have to defend ourselves. They were bad people working for bad people.'

'But we shouldn't take the law into our own hands. Should we? Or should we?'

'Why not? It's our law. Just because they've stolen control of the law doesn't make it their law. In a democracy the voters elect the legislature which makes the rules. The executive runs things according to the rules. And the judiciary decides if the rules have been broken. But everything has gone wrong. You wouldn't have got a fair trial because the same people now make the rules, run things and then decide whether the rules have been broken.'

Chapter 16

For a week they tried to forget. They constantly expected to hear on the Telescreen that the police were investigating the murder of two sprouts. Every night, Tom woke up at 3.30 a.m. and lay there waiting for Europol sprouts to burst through the front door.

But nothing happened.

No one seemed to have noticed. Or maybe no one cared.

Chapter 17

They had not, of course, been the first to stand up against the sprouts; though they were, perhaps, the first to do so quite so effectively.

There had, over the months, been many attempts at rebellion.

A group calling itself *The English Liberation Front* had made bombs out of pesticides, fertiliser, torch batteries and alarm clocks. They had not been very good at it (none of their bombs had actually gone off) and their efforts had died away for lack of supplies.

Another group, known to its members, but sadly no one else, as *Freeing England* had made a bomb and used the transmitter and receiver from a radio controlled aeroplane to detonate it. But although their bomb worked as well as could be expected they were hindered by the fact that they could only find enough explosive to make a very small bang. The breaking of a single ground floor window at a Regional Parliament building in the West Country was not regarded by EUDCE as a serious threat to the security of the State.

A third group, consisting entirely of computer specialists used their knowledge to attempt to disrupt EUDCE by feeding viruses into the organisation's computer network. Sadly for the rebels their attempt resulted in less disruption than one of the six times a day power cuts that had become accepted as part of everyday life. The group had still been arguing about the name it would use when it had disbanded.

A group of anti-fascist rebels, known as *The Blue Brigade*, had made a serious attempt to overthrow the sprouts by burning all demands for money that came from official sources. Demands from all licensing authorities were burnt on huge bonfires by crowds of cheering citizens.

'Without our money they are powerless!' claimed the leader of the rebels, who wrote a pamphlet in which he argued that the UK had been destroyed by a potent, toxic, ever-expanding tangle of gold-plated EUDCE rules and regulations. 'They can't take thousands of us to court – it will block the system!'

Sadly, this well-meant scheme of civil disobedience didn't work.

The police were instructed to pick up all the ringleaders who had burnt their bills. And they were instructed to pick up others at random. All those arrested were charged with offences under the Financial Support of Terrorism Act. They were fined heavily and sent to Africa to serve life sentences weeding parsnips. The sad result was a rapid rush to pay outstanding bills.

All further attempts to generate opposition were stifled by legislation outlawing the dissemination of information about EUDCE policies and spending policies. The publication of facts and statistics (defined as 'politically inconvenient verities') was made illegal under wide-ranging anti-terrorism legislation introduced by EUDCE under the European Securities Act.

And, as those who had known freedom, and understood what it was and what it meant, grew older and grew weary, so the number of people prepared to stand up and fight diminished. The young, who had grown up in a regimented, regulated world, knew nothing else and their expectations were low. Nothing about their world seemed wrong to them. The simplest truths and ideas are the most difficult to understand, the easiest to ignore and the hardest to do anything about.

Those among the young who were branded as suspects and destined to be nothing more than second-class citizens, did not stand up to protest; they defended and supported those who controlled the rules and regulations because that was what they had been brought up to do. They had been enslaved by their own obedience, by fear and by an understanding that this was the way it was and this was the way it was meant to be.

The bureaucrats were getting stronger every day.

Chapter 18

And then Tom and Dorothy had visitors: Gladwys Tranter and her boyfriend, Dalby Barrington.

Gladwys and Dalby both wanted to marry but EUDCE didn't approve of marriage. EUDCE's Greek born Commissioner for Social Relationships had decided that formalising relationships increased independent thinking and diminished the power of the Superstate and he had, therefore, introduced legislation barring marriage between heterosexuals, although not between homosexuals.

Gladwys Tranter was a small, dark-haired, dark-complexioned woman. Tiny, slim, alert, she was always busy, always rushing, always doing something, constantly moving; if she'd been a small animal she would have been a hamster. Or, perhaps, a sparrow. In her mid 40's, though she looked younger, she had brown hair and a boyish figure. She wore her hair short (easier to keep clean, she explained) and always wore skirts, together with blouses or jumpers. The skirts always came down to her ankles. She never wore trousers. She was a huge fan of Jane Austen and secretly read her six novels continuously; never reading anything else. She read them in sequence, as they'd been written, and when she finished the last one she immediately started to re-read the first one. She could, in the olden days, have won prizes for her specialist knowledge of this once famous, English author. As a girl she'd studied art and after graduating had worked for a while as a set designer. In her own time she'd begun to make a name for herself as a portrait artist; that had always been her first love. But then, after the final collapse of the British Parliament and the peak oil problems exacerbated by the British energy crisis of 2016, the company had gone bankrupt and the galleries where she had exhibited had all closed down. She'd tried to get work at the BBC but they weren't making drama productions any more and all their staff had to be EUDCE approved. Gladwys couldn't get EUDCE approval because she'd once been filmed by the police at an animal rights rally in Trafalgar Square. She'd thought she might be able to concentrate on her painting but no one had money to spend on art. Even the rich were turning their money into gold or silver and burying what they didn't need to spend to survive. She now eked out a small living growing a few vegetables on one of the allotments where Tom worked as a guard. Her hands, once delicate and pale and sensitive, the hands of an artist, were now brown and gnarled and covered in calluses; they were the hands of an artisan. She and Dalby had one child, a daughter, who'd had nothing whatsoever to do with them since she had married a sprout. At first this had caused Dalby and Gladwys great sadness. But now it was no longer of consequence. Their lives were too full for them to worry about this, or for them even to be aware of it.

Dalby, with whom she had lived for twenty three years, was short and liked to describe himself as solidly built, a phrase which he much preferred to oft-used alternatives such as 'chubby' and 'rotund'. The truth was that he was one of the few plump looking people on the planet who wasn't actually fat. He didn't eat all that much (no suspects ever did) but he had the sort of shape that meant that even if he'd been starving he would have looked pleasantly well-fed. He still had all his hair, which was white and curly, and he wore it so that if he'd ever worn a jacket it would have hung over his collar. Before his hair had gone white it had been reddish in colour and he still had a number of freckles to remind him of his original schooldays nickname of 'Ginger'. No one had called him that for years.

He had always been a mild-mannered man. He had been a quiet, gentle, inoffensive, inconspicuous child and he had grown up to be a quiet, gentle, inoffensive, inconspicuous man. Twenty years earlier Dalby had been a model citizen; the sort of elector of whom politicians approved. He questioned nothing. He had been the sort of person who, if he had accidentally dropped a sweet wrapper, would have gone back to pick it up and chased it around in the wind to make sure he managed to collect it. (In truth, on one occasion he had narrowly escaped being run over after chasing a breeze-blown toffee wrapper into oncoming traffic.)

But he had changed. He had begun to feel an unusual feeling stirring within him. The feeling was rage and because he'd never felt that way before he didn't immediately understand what it was that he was feeling.

Several things had triggered this change in Dalby's demeanour.

First, back in the days when suspects still had motor cars and a modest petrol ration, a council workman had erected a bus stop in the pavement right in front of Dalby's driveway. The bus stop's position meant that Dalby could no longer get his car in and out of his driveway. Since his car had been out of the driveway when the sign was erected he had to leave it parked on the street near the bus stop. This had, within weeks, resulted in seven parking tickets and twice as many letters of protest and complaint to the relevant EUDCE officer in Dijon (all of which had, of course, been completely ignored).

Then a routine visit from a sprout (who'd turned up on an annual visit to photograph the inside of their house, and its contents) had resulted in the confiscation of Dalby's entire home, together with its contents.

The sprout had found a book called *England Our England* amidst a shelf full of otherwise harmless volumes and there had been an awful row about it. Even mentioning England had been a serious offence for years. Having a book in your home with the forbidden word in the title was about as serious an offence as could be imagined.

Dorothy and Tom had invited Gladwys and Dalby for coffee. In the old days it would have probably been a dinner party. But no one had dinner parties any more. Most people could only just afford to feed themselves. The idea of giving food to friends and acquaintances had, among suspects, long been regarded as absurd.

'So, tell us about your new job,' said Dorothy, when their visitors had been welcomed and coffee had been served.

Dalby had for some time earned a small living as a rat catcher. But, like everyone they knew, he needed a second job. And he'd recently acquired one.

'He's a Relinquished Arboreal Cotyledon Accruement Specialist.' Gladwys blushed. 'It sounds much grander than it is,' she added.

'What's one of those do?' asked Tom.

'I go round with a brush and a wheelbarrow and sweep up fallen leaves,' said Dalby. 'It's seasonal work but I've been given a full time contract.'

'But there aren't any trees left,' Tom pointed out. Streets and parks had long since been stripped of their trees by homeowners looking for wood to burn.

'There are quite a few senior Regional Parliament officers who still have trees in their gardens,' explained Dalby. 'I look after those. A leaf here, a leaf there.'

'Ah.'

'They don't like the leaves lying around.'

'No, I suppose not. Untidy. What's your sprout like?' asked Tom. Every working suspect worked directly under the supervision of a sprout.

'He isn't too bright. I think he probably struggled at school with his one times table. Today his official title is Tree Supervisor and his main job is to keep a record of any new trees appearing.'

'That must be exhausting.'

'I think he lives in hope.'

They sat in silence for a while.

It was Tom who broke the silence.

'You both seem preoccupied.' Tom was often blunter than Dorothy in social situations. 'What's up?' he asked. He looked at Gladwys and then at Dalby. 'Would you like more coffee?' he added, trying to lighten the question.

Gladwys looked at Dalby who thought for a moment, trying to decide if it would be ruder to say 'no', and perhaps imply that the coffee didn't taste too good, or to say 'yes' and deprive Tom and Dorothy of another spoonful of their carefully self-rationed stash of instant coffee. The coffee, being not too far past its official 'best before' date still tasted of coffee. If you closed your eyes you knew what you were drinking.

'I will have another cup, please,' said Dalby, handing up his cup. 'It's excellent.' He looked up at Tom. 'You don't supplement with ground acorns do you?' It had become commonplace to make coffee stocks last longer by mixing instant coffee with ground acorns.

'We used to,' admitted Tom. 'But since they chopped down all the oak trees we haven't been able to get any acorns.' Bizarrely, one black market salesman had offered them ground acorns at twice the price of instant coffee.

'True enough,' nodded Dalby.

'So, what's happened?' asked Tom, quietly. He refilled Dalby's cup and turned to the two women. 'No one else for a refill?' They both shook their heads.

Dalby and Gladwys looked at each other.

***

Like everyone else they had learned to be careful about what they wrote, whom they saw and what they said (wherever they were when they said it). These precautions were second nature now. Caution was the default setting for suspects. Suspects had even become careful about what they thought. It had become impossible to conceive of anything being beyond the reach of the sprouts. Even the absurd and the impossible were now probably possible. Who knew? The Dalbys were close friends with Tom and Dorothy. But even so you could never really be sure. Not, sure sure.

Every patriotic European had for years been encouraged to regard it as his or her duty to inform the authorities of any behaviour which could in any way be described as suspicious. A woman in what had once been Dover in Kent, but what was now officially part of a region of Northern France, reported a neighbour simply because he had a parcel delivered to his door. A woman in what had once been Manchester reported that a man living in a nearby flat had lingerie hanging on his washing line, although he supposedly lived alone. Denunciation was everywhere.

It was easy for sneaks or snoops to operate and many did so openly. The more successful among them proudly wore 'good surveillance' badges, much as boy scouts had worn badges in the days when the Boy Scout movement was a popular way to guide the energy and enthusiasm of young boys. The badges carried the slogan 'Building a Caring, Thoughtful Society'. Some of the keenest citizens had equipped themselves with telescopes or binoculars to improve their ability to spy on those around them. Tom knew of two men in nearby streets who had infra-red binoculars. Both stayed up at night to watch for illegal activities in the streets below. Any sneak whose reports resulted in a neighbour being deported received a relatively huge bonus. People accused of lesser crimes would be fined, with 10% of the fine going to the sneak who had made the report. Any suspect who couldn't afford a fine but who owned property would have to sign over some of the equity in their home. This meant that hundreds of thousands of home-owners were gradually losing ownership of their properties and having to pay rent. (Once again, the sneaks involved received a percentage of the money collected.) As far as sneaks were concerned the real beauty of the system was that they didn't have to be right. An accusation was, generally speaking, regarded as being just as significant as a conviction might have been a few decades earlier. Sneaking kept everyone on their toes. Officially the sneaks (or snitches as they were sometimes called) were known as Specialist Information Relocation Experts.

The system had begun with people being encouraged to report their neighbours to the authorities. In the early days, people telephoned to report that their neighbours weren't putting out their rubbish on the right day. When rubbish collections were stopped completely they telephoned to report that their neighbours had left rubbish in the street instead of sorting it and carrying it to the various authorised dumps. When the authorities realised that an increasing number of snoops were staying up at night in order to observe their neighbours they abandoned official patrols. The informal snooper system was, they discovered, cheaper and much more effective.

Many EUDCE departments gave rewards to informers (some, such as the Revenue collectors, gave a percentage of whatever money was recovered and some awarded points which could be exchanged for holidays or clothing coupons. No one ever checked or investigated allegations. For EUDCE the bonus was that the system kept suspects fearful and suspicious of one another. The generic slogan for the system was 'Together Our Communities Will Build a Caring, Thoughtful Society'.

A Good Neighbour Initiative, introduced and sponsored by the Regional Parliament, gave Good Neighbours 1,000 citizenship points for every neighbour they denounced. The Regional Parliament claimed that a majority of the population had registered for the Good Neighbour initiative and had each made at least five reports in the preceding six week period. A spokesman for the Parliament expressed dismay at the relative failure of the scheme when compared to similar schemes in other parts of the Union. Good Neighbours were encouraged to report anyone they knew who hadn't registered for the scheme or who had expressed disapproval. Collect enough points and you could get on Reality Television and, if you won, be given a lifetime job contract as a Trusty.

Reality television programmes were broadcast constantly on the Telescreen. The most popular programme allowed viewers to vote on which contestant should die (and how they should die). Drawing and quartering was popular, as was pulling apart with horses. All live on the Telescreen, of course. A revised version of the long running Big

Brother programme had been running for five years. One contestant, who had been in the new Big Brother programme since the beginning of the series, had conceived and given birth to three children in the Big Brother house. All live on the Telescreen. There were, of course, three different fathers. The Telescreen producers had auctioned off the children (a pop singer had bought two) and invited viewers to choose the father of the woman's next baby.

***

It was Dalby who found the courage to speak.

'We have our weekly Legacy Achievement Awareness Scrutineering in the morning,' he said.

A month earlier both Dalby and Gladwys had failed a spot check in the street and part of the automatic punishment was that they now had to be checked once a week for ten weeks. If one of them failed just one of these examinations both of them would automatically be found guilty of 'Poor Citizenship'.

Every piece of news chosen by the editors for broadcast on the Telescreen was deemed a 'European Legacy' and suspects were, therefore, expected to take careful note of everything that appeared. If, when asked questions relating to the previous week's telecasts, suspects failed to achieve an acceptable score they were in serious trouble. Suspects who were being tested and who failed to answer enough questions accurately didn't receive any loyalty credits. And suspects who were being tested and who didn't acquire loyalty credits couldn't buy food. Life sometimes seemed complicated.

Built into the system there was, of course, a great deal of opportunity for the Scrutineers to fail suspects who should have passed, and to pass suspects who should have failed. Since virtually no suspects had any wealth to speak of, it was common for sprouts to demand sexual favours from suspect victims or their relatives. Most suspects hated paying the licence fee. ('Why should we pay for propaganda?' they asked.) But more, even than that, they hated having to prove that they had watched the stuff

'It's garbage,' said Dalby. 'They call it news but it's just propaganda. We have to pay to receive it. And then they test us to make sure we've watched it.' He put his head in his hands.

'It's unfair,' said Gladwys. 'It's compulsory to have a Telescreen and compulsory to pay a licence fee to watch programmes you don't want to watch and then they test you to make sure you've been watching, and if you haven't they punish you.'

'Why don't we test you?' suggested Tom, softly. 'Between us Dorothy and I probably know most of what's been on the Telescreen this week.' He thought for a few moments. 'Here's one. What is the current punishment for putting your rubbish in the wrong recycling bin at an authorised collecting centre?'

Dalby frowned and thought hard. 'Isn't it still deportation?'

'No, afraid not. It went up this week. It's now double deportation.'

'What on earth is double deportation? How can you be deported twice?'

'They've changed it because there's been a boom in the number of people believing in reincarnation,' explained Tom. 'The idea is that when you come back the next time you get deported again.'

'But how on earth do they know you've been reincarnated?' asked Dalby. 'What if you come back as a wasp or a hedgehog?'

'Don't ask me,' said Tom. 'I don't make this stuff up. I'm just reporting what they said on the Telescreen.'

'OK,' sighed Dalby.

'EUDCE has started a new sex industry course on the Telescreen...,' Dorothy began.

'Oh, I saw that,' said Gladwys. 'It's called *How to be a Hooker*'. At the end of the course you send in a eurocheque for your diploma and degree. Then you're entitled to work as a prostitute and pay a 30% reduced fine if the police catch you.'

'Spot on,' agreed Dorothy. 'And don't forget the Telescreen is also running public service advertisements for a new chain of brothels called *Tarts'R'Us*.'

'I've got a question for you,' said Tom. 'An 18-year-old youth was arrested and deported this week for the crime of homosexual bigotry. Can you tell me precisely what he did?'

'Oh, I saw this one,' said Dalby. 'He refused his Compulsory Community Youth Homosexual Experience didn't he?' He shook his head in disbelief 'I'm so pleased they brought that law in after I reached 21.'

'You know that ministerial appointments in the Regional Parliament have been sponsored for some years?' said Tom.

'Yes, of course.' replied Gladwys. 'You mean, things like the

Ford Transport Minister, the Marlborough Minister of Health and the McDonald Minister of Healthy Eating?'

'Absolutely. So, can you name the person who was this week appointed McCann Regional Minister of Child Supervision?'

Gladwys and Dalby thought hard. 'Gary Glitter? Jonathan King?'

Tom shook his head. 'I don't even know if those two are still alive!' he admitted.

'No idea,' Dalby and Gladwys admitted eventually.

'They appointed a Turkish woman who has 16 children on the grounds that she has more experience of child supervision than anyone else in Europe.'

Unsurprised by this, Dalby and Gladwys nodded.

'A new world record in beheading was set this week by an executionist in Arizona. Can you tell me how many heads he chopped off in ten minutes?'

'I think I heard about this,' said Dalby. 'It was 37 wasn't it?'

'I think it was 37,' agreed Gladwys. She shuddered. 'It was live on the Telescreen but I couldn't watch it. They kept showing the whole thing over and over again. I watched the first minute the first time but after that I had to turn away. All those heads, just rolling around on the floor.'

'Thirty seven is right,' said Tom.

'How do you know the answers to all this stuff.' demanded Dalby.

'I'm asking the questions,' Tom pointed out. 'And I'm only asking questions to which I know the answers.' He paused, and thought for a moment, trying to recall something else he could ask. 'On the same subject, which country's Olympic Committee is insisting that executions are introduced as a main event at the next Olympics?'

'The Chinese?' suggested Gladwys.

'No, it isn't,' said Dalby firmly. 'It's the Americans.'

'Dead right,' agreed Tom. 'This next one is a history question,' he went on. 'But they ask these sometimes if they've been used on the Telescreen. I saw this in a quiz programme. Who were the first?'

'I know the answer to this one too,' said Gladwys excitedly. 'It was Dame Ulrika Johnson and Lord Piers Morgan, wasn't it?'

'Brilliant!' said Tom.

'I'm going to have to rely on you,' said Dalby to his wife, rather wearily. 'I just don't seem able to absorb this stuff.'

'Well I think you're both doing brilliantly,' said Dorothy, who still retained at least some of her optimism and who believed firmly in the power of positive thinking. 'You should sail through.'

'It's the bloody mindlessness of it,' said Dalby, gloomily. 'And when they're in the flat you're constantly on edge, waiting for them to find something else to do you for.' After their house had been confiscated he and Gladwys had moved into a small flat in a low-rent high rise building. Their flat was on the sixteenth floor. Since the lift had not been working for several years they had got into the habit of leaving the sixteenth floor only once or twice a week.

'Some of the sprouts we've seen recently have been really fat,' said Gladwys. 'I read somewhere that they all claim that they have hormonal problems. But they can't all be ill can they?'

'They're just fat and greedy,' said Tom. 'If that's a medical condition then they're ill.'

'I'm afraid we keep hoping one of them will have a heart attack climbing the stairs,' said Gladwys.

'Or fall down the stairs!' laughed Dalby. Then the laughter suddenly stopped as he remembered something. He leant across towards Tom and lowered his voice. 'We still haven't got a gate on our staircase.' He stopped and thought for a while. 'Or a safety harness. Do you happen to know what the penalty is for not having a properly protected staircase? The staircase isn't inside our flat so it's our landlord's responsibility, of course. But even so...'

'We don't have a gate either,' said Tom.

'Or a safety harness,' added Dorothy.

'We had a EUDCE-approved Home Safety Advisory Consultant round to give us a quote,' said Tom. 'We'll never be able to afford what he wanted.' He shrugged sadly.

'Can't you get someone else to give you a quote? Some other firm?'

Tom shook his head. 'There's only one firm of Home Safety Advisory Consultants licensed in this region,' he said.

'That doesn't seem right,' said Dalby. 'There's no competition for anything these days.'

'EUDCE sells exclusive licences,' said Tom. 'They can charge more for exclusive licences. Officially, there's only one firm of plumbers in this region.'

EUDCE sold licences to everyone, and for everything imaginable. People who had for years done their jobs, practised their professions, effectively, efficiently, responsibly and fairly, suddenly found that they were ordered to take new tests, pass new examinations and (this the key) obtain new licences for which they had to pay hefty, annual fees. The money was paid to a bunch of EUDCE authorised eurocratic regulators so that they could set more tests, introduce more licences and collect more fees. EUDCE had become a self-perpetuating, self-funding leech, sucking the life-blood both from the hard-working professionals and from the citizens who relied upon the services they provided.

To pay for their licences the regulated workers had to increase their fees and in order to find the time to speak to the regulators, and to take the examinations required of them, they had to reduce the quality of the service they provided. Everything sank to the lowest common denominator. Fees went up, service went down. Every professional, every tradesman in every business and every trade, had to be regulated and had to pay for the privilege of being licensed.

'We know a plumber who does work privately,' whispered Dorothy. 'If you ever need to get in touch with him, let us know. He's brilliant with dripping taps, blocked drains – that sort of thing.'

'We're terrified that we'll have a Residential Placement Officer come round,' said Dalby. 'Several of the people in our building have been forced to take in people. An old lady who lives on the floor below us now has five Turks living with her. I met her on the landing the other day. She looked terrible. They ate her cat the first night they were there. Just killed it, cooked it and ate it. She has no more rooms than we have. Just one living room and one bedroom. A tiny kitchenette and a tiny bathroom.'

There was a housing shortage. This was partly a result of the very active pro-immigration policy introduced by EUDCE, and partly a result of the fact that houses built in the .latter part of the 20th century had been shoddily made and were falling down at a calamitous rate. There were no materials for building new houses or for repairing old ones. The result was that householders were forced to share their accommodation.

'She can't complain, of course,' said Gladwys. 'They'd charge her with aggravated racism and send her to an Involuntary Euthanasia Clinic.' Suspects over the age of 60 who were arrested weren't exported. They were considered likely to be too unfit to work in the fields and were, therefore, sent to one of EUDCE's Involuntary Euthanasia Clinics.

'I thought the immigrants were all leaving, all going back home,' said Dorothy. 'But for every one who leaves another dozen now seem to arrive.'

'It's the EUDCE Racial Amalgamation Policy,' explained Tom. 'The aim is to homogenise the European population.'

'But why do these people still come here?' demanded Dalby.

'There's no work, little food, overcrowded housing and a completely broken-down infrastructure. The trains run when there's enough diesel or coal to move them. The hospitals are more or less closed to anyone who isn't a sprout.'

'EUDCE gives low-grade trusty jobs to Turks, Romanians, Latvians, Croatians, Estonians, Poles and so on,' explained Tom.

'And the Maltese too.' He hesitated. 'What the hell do you call people from Malta?'

'Maltesers I suppose,' said Dorothy.

'Yes, I suppose so,' replied Tom. 'And they give resettlement grants to thousands more. They have huge recruiting campaigns. A Pole I know told me he got a grant of 5,000 euros to come here. If he goes back within 12 months he has to give back the grant. The sprouts hope that a few of them will find girls of English origin, stay here, have children, and settle down. It's part of their Social Integration Policy.'

'I didn't know that,' said Dalby. 'I don't suppose we can get grants to go somewhere else?'

'Sadly no,' said Tom. 'Those of English origin aren't allowed to apply for grants.'

They all sat glumly in silence for a while.

'I could come round and pretend to be living in your flat,' said Tom. 'They might not report you for undercrowding if you have another adult living with you.'

'That wouldn't work,' said Dorothy. 'They'd want to see your papers – something to prove that you're registered as living there.'

'I could get some false papers,' said Tom. 'I know a guy who makes quite good ones. He used to work for the Government, when we last had one.'

'You couldn't get them by tomorrow,' Dorothy pointed out.

'No,' admitted Tom sadly.

The four of them sat in silence.

'Have you noticed that most of the sprouts come from Romania, Turkey and Israel these days,' said Dorothy.

'I never understood how Israel came to be a member of EUDCE,' said Gladwys.

'They were in the Eurovision Song Contest and so they had fast-tracked membership to EUDCE,' said Dorothy.

Israel hadn't been the only surprise. After eight African nations were officially accepted as fully integrated regions of the United States of Europe it was widely agreed that EUDCE had become China's main competitor for world dominance – the USA having been relegated to the status of also-ran.

'I heard EUDCE is planning to appoint a lot of new low-level sprouts from Latvia,' said Gladwys. 'More homogenisation, I suppose.'

'Did you hear that they're phasing out English?' said Tom.

Dalby and Gladwys looked at him.

'A friend of mine who used to work as a cleaner at the BBC told me that the commissioners have decided that EUDCE's two official languages are to be Turkish and French. We're all going to be given two years to learn one or the other. After that all other languages will be illegal.'

This was clearly a shock to both Dalby and Gladwys.

'Are you sure?'

'It was discussed at a BBC Allegiance Meeting.'

The BBC was, as it had been even before the British Broadcasting Corporation became the Brussels Broadcasting Corporation (a change that involved a change of notepaper rather than any change in underlying policy matters), the unofficial propaganda machine for EUDCE. Every morning BBC staff at all its studios were expected to attend morning Allegiance Meetings where, in a daily ceremony known to outsiders as 'morning prayers', they would swear loyalty to the European project and the United States of Europe.

'They've been planning it for ages,' said Tom.

'When are they bringing that in?' asked Dalby.

Tom shrugged. 'Not sure,' he said. 'My friend reached her 60th birthday so they fired her. No pension, no watch, no party, no thanks. Just 'Don't bother coming in on Monday.' She's opening up a herbal clinic in her living room. But it means we don't have access to their waste paper basket any more.'

'I could just do with a nice cup of tea!'

Everyone turned. Tom's aunt was standing in the doorway. 'I had a nap,' she said. She was wearing a long, baggy, grey cardigan over an ankle length pale pink nightdress and holding Tabatha in her arms. She stifled a yawn. 'I take lots of naps. I think I may be addicted to them. This nightie used to be cream but I washed it with a pair of Dorothy's red knickers and now it's pink.'

'You know my aunt, don't you?' said Tom to Dalby and Gladwys.

They said they did. 'Auntie, this is Dalby and Gladwys.'

'Hello. Everyone thinks I'm potty,' said Tom's aunt, waving to Dalby and Gladwys. 'But I'm as sane as a ferret. Ask me the name of the last Prime Minister. That's what the man at the hospital kept asking me.'

No one spoke.

'Go on, ask me,' insisted Tom's aunt.

'What's the name of the Prime Minister?' asked Dalby.

Tom's aunt stared at him and then grinned broadly. 'Don't have the foggiest,' she said. 'And I don't give a fig. There hasn't been a decent one since Winston Churchill. Most of them have been traitors.'

Tom looked at his aunt. He sometimes wondered whether she had Alzheimer's disease at all, or whether she used the label as a convenient screen behind which she could hide when she didn't want to be bothered by the world around her. 'I'll make you a cup of tea, Aunt,' he said. His aunt didn't like coffee.

'Make sure it's a nice one,' she told him. 'Do you know the funny thing is that although my nightie is now pink Dorothy's knickers are still as red as they ever were.'

'I suppose we'd better be going,' said Dalby, standing up. Gladwys stood up too.

'Don't go just because of me,' said Tom's aunt. 'I don't have fits or do anything antisocial.' She smiled at them. When she smiled it was almost impossible to dislike her or to be cross with her. 'I won't mention knickers again.'

'No, no,' said Dalby, embarrassed. 'It's not because of you. We were just going anyway. We have to get up early in the morning.'

'Are you going somewhere nice or do you have the sprouts coming round?' asked Tom's aunt.

'The sprouts are coming,' replied Gladwys.

'Don't be frightened of them,' insisted Tom's aunt. 'Politeness is all very well but it doesn't put butter on parsnips. We had the sprouts here.'

'Did you?' said Gladwys. She turned to Dorothy. 'You didn't say.'

'They were probably too shy to mention it,' said Tom's aunt. 'We had two. They came to look at the labels.'

'Strewth,' said Dalby. 'I hate the label inspectors. They always manage to find something. Last time they visited, one found an old pair of sunglasses that didn't have a label on them. We got an official warning.'

'And they took the sunglasses away with them,' added Gladwys.

'They always take something with them,' said Tom.

'We killed ours,' said Tom's aunt. No one spoke.

No one breathed.

No one moved.

Chapter 19

There are, Tom realised, different types of silence. This was the deepest, quietest silence he had ever heard. Some silences aren't really silences at all. People stop talking but they do other things that make other noises. They clink teacups, they rustle pieces of paper, they blow their noses, they clear their throats, they scratch their heads, they recross their legs.

This was a true silence. A time without sound. The room was so silent that Tom could hear an alarm clock ticking in the house next door. He could hear four people breathing. He could feel his heart beating so fast he felt sure that it would explode. He laughed nervously and waved a hand, as though to suggest that this was just his aunt's craziness talking.

'Both of them,' said Tom's aunt, who seemed unaware that her words had had such an effect. She lowered her voice, as though about to share a secret. 'It's very easy,' she added, confidentially. 'You just hit them with a frying pan.'

Everyone in the room looked at her. Two of the people in the room didn't really believe what they'd heard. The other two didn't want to believe that they'd heard it.

'You hit them with a frying pan,' she repeated. She made a hitting movement with her right hand; her fingers formed into a fist as though holding the handle of a frying pan. She looked around at the open mouths and bewildered, slightly frightened faces. 'One just fell down the stairs so we didn't really kill that one. But we finished him off. And we killed the other one with the frying pan,' she said. She turned to Tom. 'We should put two notches in the frying pan handle,' she said.

Dalby looked at Tom and then at Dorothy. He sat down again. Gladwys sat down too.

'She's not joking is she?' said Dalby. He looked first at Tom and then at Dorothy.

'No,' said Tom very softly. This was, he felt, the moment of truth. They were about to find out just how much they could trust their visitors. He took a deep breath. 'No, she's not joking.'

'What did you do with the bodies?' asked Gladwys.

'We took them to the hospital,' said Dorothy. 'We put them on gurneys, those flat half-stretcher half-trolley things they have in hospitals, and left both of them in a corridor.'

'When was this?'
'Last Thursday.'
'Five days ago?' Tom nodded.
'And nothing has happened?'
He shook his head.
'The police haven't been round?'
'No.'
'Do you think you got away with it?'
'Hope so,' said Dorothy.
'Why haven't we heard anything about it?' asked Gladwys. 'Has it been on the Telescreen?'
'Maybe the police are stupid,' said Dalby.
'Maybe they are,' said Tom firmly. 'They rely on sneaks and computers to do everything for them. Most of them never leave their offices. But unless computers are programmed they don't think round corners. No sprout has been murdered for years and so my guess is that they wouldn't consider it as a possibility.' He hesitated. 'The only other explanation I can think of is that they know but aren't doing anything about it because they're too nervous to admit that two sprouts got killed. Sprouts go into people's homes all day long. They're armed only with their arrogance and the knowledge that we're terrified of them. The commissioners wouldn't want suspects to know that sprouts were vulnerable. And they certainly wouldn't want the sprouts to know.'
'And we helped confuse the issue by putting identification tags on the two bodies we left in the hospital,' Dorothy reminded Tom. 'It made it all look like an official cock-up.'
'That was a brilliant touch,' agreed Tom. He explained how Dorothy had done this.
Tom's aunt, who was bored by all this talk, leapt up and went to the cupboard under the sink. She pulled out the frying pan. 'We hit them with this!' she told the two visitors, waving the frying pan in the air around their heads. 'This is what we used.' She brandished the frying pan as she had done when hitting the sprout. 'Whoosh!' she said.
'Was it easy?' asked Gladwys.
'Getting rid of the bodies?'

'No. Killing them?'

'That was surprisingly easy,' said Tom. 'One of the sprouts fell down the stairs. That was an accident. We were standing on the landing. He was poking me in the chest with his finger, you know the way sprouts do, really hard, and it was hurting me so I stepped aside. The next time he prodded I wasn't there and he went down the stairs. He didn't die straight away but it was pretty clear he was pretty badly hurt. The other one threatened to have the three of us deported. He wouldn't listen to reason. He knew it wasn't my fault but he wouldn't listen to me. He said I'd pushed the other sprout.' He lowered his voice. 'I didn't have any choice,' he said, almost whispering.

For a while no one spoke.

'I'd do it again,' said Tom. 'It was the right thing to do. The killing was easy. It was getting rid of the bodies that was tricky.'

Once again, no one spoke.

'Are you terribly shocked?' Dorothy asked Gladwys.

Gladwys looked at Dalby. They both looked towards Dorothy. 'No,' said Gladwys. 'Not shocked.' She thought again. 'Not shocked at all,' she said very quietly.

'I would describe myself as sympathetic and interested,' said Dalby, quietly. 'Very interested. Very sympathetic.'

'Did you have to hit the one you killed very much?' asked Gladwys.

'A few times,' nodded Tom. 'Quite hard. Yes, quite hard.'

'Boof!' said his aunt. She raised the frying pan, which she was still holding, and then brought it down fast. She smiled at them.

'Did your aunt...?' asked Dalby.

'Yes,' admitted Tom. He half smiled. 'She turned out to be surprisingly good at it.' He swallowed. 'I had no choice,' he said. 'And I don't think what I did was wrong.' He rubbed a hand through what was left of his hair. 'EUDCE has taken over our country, our culture, our past, our present, our future, our democracy and our freedom. They haven't left us anything. The people who represent the new State, the sprouts, may not have been responsible for creating the EUDCE concept but they're responsible for what is happening to us. We can't beat a system because it doesn't really exist; it's a plan, a notion, a badness. All we can do is chop off the arms and legs; the beasts who do the State's bidding. We can't reach the commissioners because they've all locked themselves away in

Brussels.'

'But the sprouts are here with us every day,' said Dalby.

'If you got away with it...,' began Gladwys.

'Maybe others could too...,' Dalby continued the thought.

'I've got a bottle of potato wine,' said Tom, suddenly. He stood up. 'I was keeping it for Christmas but I have a feeling this is a special occasion too.'

'I'll get some glasses,' said Dorothy.

When Tom had opened the potato wine and filled all the glasses the questions came thick and fast. Where exactly did you put the bodies? How did you get them there? Do you really think you'll get away with it? Do you think we could get rid of the Telescreen license guy? The planning man? The idiot from the valuation office who comes round to photograph everything inside the house? The income tax inspector?'

And then, finally.

'Can you help us get rid of the sprouts who are coming to see us tomorrow?'

'Oh, you'll pass the test with flying colours,' said Tom. He tried to sound more reassuring than he felt.

'It isn't the test that really worries us,' said Gladwys. 'We're doing what we can to help ourselves so it isn't entirely out of our hands. What really worries us is the fear that they're going to make us take lodgers.'

'It's a tiny flat,' explained Dalby. 'There's hardly room for the two of us.'

'They took our last home just about a year ago,' said Gladwys.

'Just confiscated it. We'd worked for years to make it nice.' There were tears in her eyes. 'I don't think I've got the strength to move again. And, besides, where would we go?'

'We'll help you,' promised Dorothy. She looked at Tom. He nodded.

'We've got a heavy saucepan,' said Dalby with a nervous smile.

'And a frying pan,' said Gladwys.

They all sipped their potato wine.

'Why are you doing this for us?' asked Dalby eventually.

'Because we have to stick together,' said Dorothy. 'We have to help one another.'

'But you're putting yourselves at risk.'

'If you don't take risks to help your friends then there isn't much to life is there?' said Tom. 'We'll come over with the trailer in the morning.' He thought for a moment. 'I might be able to get hold of a bigger one. I know a chap who has one of the allotments. He's getting old and his trailer is too big for him. It's heavy but strong. Too big for his needs. I've seen him eyeing mine rather enviously. I'll see if he wants to trade.' He paused again and then looked at Dalby. 'Are you still catching rats?'

Dalby nodded. He had earned a living catching rats for a long time. The areas where suspects lived were thick with them.

'Can you get a couple of dozen of dead ones by tomorrow?'

'No problem.'

'More if you can manage it,' said Tom. 'We might need quite a few.'

Chapter 20

The sprouts who turned up to question Dalby and Gladwys were both Turkish. They spoke English very slowly and deliberately, having to weigh each word before delivering it. One of the sprouts was very short and very fat. The other was shorter and even fatter. The thinnest of the two wore a thin black moustache. The fatter of the two was clean shaven and bald. The thinner was a keen collector of barbed wire. He had 79 one metre stretches fastened onto heavy corkboards and fixed to the wall in his bedroom. The fatter was a collector of car numbers. He had filled eight notebooks.

'Who is these persons?' demanded the sprout with the moustache, looking at Tom, Dorothy and Tom's aunt who was holding her cat.

'Just friends,' replied Dalby.

'Visitors,' said Gladwys.

'We came to help with some cooking,' said Tom, holding up the frying pan he was holding. Dorothy held up a heavy iron wok she'd found. They were both still shocked by the circumstances in which their friends were living. The tower block where Dalby and Gladwys had their flat was worse than anything they'd ever seen before. It was, thought Tom, like something out of the sort of science fiction movie that was popular back in the 20th century.

'You are not to be having visitors when we are coming,' said the bald sprout. 'Even when they are also old.' He had clearly put on weight since he'd been given his suit. It bulged, threateningly, in all the usual places. He wagged a plump finger at Dorothy, Tom and Tom's aunt. 'These are all suspects, no?'

'Yes,' said Tom. To his own surprise he did not feel in the slightest bit nervous. It occurred to him, in a fleeting instant of comprehension, that it is confidence which wins battles but that in the end it doesn't much matter whether the confidence is based on the solid rocks of knowledge and accomplishment or the shifting, tremulous sands of hope and expectation.

The bald sprout looked them up and down contemptuously and then looked away, ignoring them now. 'I am a Residential Placement Officer,' he said pompously. He looked around, allowing time for this information to sink in.

Gladwys started to cry.

'I thought you would be Scrutineers,' said Dalby.

'Not us,' said the bald sprout, delighting in Dalby's obvious discomfort. 'You expect them so we come instead.' He looked around him. 'You have much rooms in here.'

'It's a very small flat,' said Dalby. 'Just two rooms.'

'Plenty of spaces for refugees,' insisted the sprout. 'Six I think.'

'No!' cried Gladwys. 'You can't! Where can we put six extra people? We have one bedroom and one living room.'

The bald sprout shrugged. 'This is my decision,' he said. 'They come to you Saturday. You will be responsible for providing food and other needs of theirs.'

'We hardly have enough to eat ourselves,' said Dalby.

'You will have six refugees,' the sprout said again making it clear that this was a statement of fact and not a potential subject for discussion. He turned and beamed at Gladwys. 'All men I think. Then you have seven men to live with. Maybe you make them very, very welcome?' He reached out and squeezed one of Gladwys's breasts. 'Small but nice,' he said. 'Very strong.'

'Firm,' said his colleague, correcting him. 'You mean 'very firm'?'

'How do you know? demanded the first sprout. 'Have you felt?'

'No,' admitted the second sprout.

'Can we appeal this decision?' asked Dalby, who was red-faced with anger.

The baldest sprout laughed and turned to his colleague. He said something in what was presumably Turkish, though no one else in the room knew that for sure since Turkish was merely one of many languages they did not understand. The two sprouts both laughed. 'You have no appeal,' sneered the one with the moustache. 'You are just scum. We alone decide.'

The other sprout shrugged again, to show that none of this was really of interest to him. Followed by his colleague he headed into the tiny kitchen. And as he did so Tom, who was standing by the door which led into the kitchen, hit him hard on the head. The sprout sank to the ground without a sound. His colleague, who was following him a pace behind, started to say something but before he could get any words out he too collapsed; felled by a blow from the heavy iron wok wielded by Dorothy. Because the wok had no proper handle Dorothy had to grip it by one of the small handles built into the edge. The wok wasn't the best of blunt instruments but, being made of solid iron, it was very heavy and effective.

'Yes!' cried Tom's aunt excitedly. 'Now it's my turn!' She grabbed the wok from Dorothy and used it to batter the fallen sprout just as Tom delivered a second blow to the head of the first sprout.

The killing was all over in less than two minutes.

'Are they dead?' whispered Gladwys.

'I think we should help a little,' said Dalby. 'I feel guilty about letting you do everything.' He took the frying pan from Tom and smashed it down onto the first sprout's head. Then Gladwys took it from him and used it to smash the second sprout's skull. Tom's aunt was still clutching the wok and seemed unwilling to give it up.

'Now we are all in this together,' said Dalby. He was breathing heavily, though this was probably more from anxiety than physical effort.

'Are they both dead?' asked Gladwys again.

Tom bent down and felt for pulses. 'They're both dead,' he said. He thought he sounded much calmer than he felt.

'That was damned good fun!' said his aunt. 'Are there any more?' She lifted up the wok and brought it crashing down onto an imaginary third victim.

'No, auntie,' said Tom, putting a soothing hand on her arm and gently taking the wok out of her grasp. 'That's enough for today.'

'Oh bugger,' said his aunt, obviously disappointed.

'Now we have to get rid of the bodies,' said Dalby. He was very pale.

'Shall we take them to the hospital?' asked Gladwys. 'And get rid of them the way you got rid of your two?'

'No,' said Tom. He was bending down removing identification papers from the two men's pockets. 'I think the hospital is too risky to use a second time.'

'Should we keep those?' asked Dalby, pointing to the papers and roaming licences Tom held.

'No,' replied Tom. 'It's far too risky. Do you have a fireplace? A stove?'

Dalby nodded.

'Show me,' said Tom, who wanted to see the papers burn. Dalby showed him their stove. 'It's out. We don't have much wood. We only light it when the weather is freezing.'

Tom put the papers into the stove, took out a cigarette lighter, and set fire to them. When they'd finished burning he used a fork to break up the charred paper and stir the ashes.

'So what are we going to do with the bodies?' asked Gladwys. She sounded a little panicky. 'We can't keep them here!'

'We could get some acid and dissolve them,' suggested Dalby. 'Or take them to a EUDCE rubbish tip.'

'They've got dozens of different sectors there,' Gladwys pointed out. 'Where do you put human bodies? You can hardly toss them in the Green Bottle Bank or the Used Sandals Bank.'

'We're going to strip them and toss both the bodies and the clothes down the rubbish chute on your landing,' said Tom. 'Then we'll go downstairs, put the bodies into the trailer on the back of my bicycle and move them somewhere else.' Earlier that day Tom had acquired the bigger trailer for his bicycle. It was plenty big enough to carry two bodies.

'Where to?' asked Gladwys.

'Dunno yet,' said Tom. He turned to Dalby. 'Where are the rats?'

'In a sack in the hall cupboard.'

'How many?'

'Eighty or so.'

'Strewth. You killed that many rats in one evening?' Dalby nodded.

'Do they ever empty the skip at the bottom of your rubbish chute?'

'No. It's been overflowing for years.'

'Do you get any scavengers?'

'Occasionally,' said Dalby. 'But not even scavengers can get much out of the rubbish thrown away here.'

'OK,' said Tom. 'So, we push the two sprouts down the rubbish chute and then we go down and pick them up. Bring the rats with you when we've dumped the two bodies.'

'Where did you leave your bike and the trailer?' asked Dalby. He'd opened their front door and was dragging the first sprout towards the rubbish chute. 'You didn't leave it outside did you? If you did it will have gone long ago.'

'I hauled it up to the second floor landing,' said Tom, who was dragging the second sprout.

'I hope it's still there,' said Dalby. 'This is a rough neighbourhood.' He paused, pushed open the hatch to the rubbish chute and looked inside. He could see nothing but the remains of the rubbish that had been dumped down it most recently.

'It will be,' said Tom confidently. He heaved one of the bodies up to the chute and, with Dalby's help, heaved it through the hatch. They did the same with the second one.

And then they headed for the door which led from the landing down the stairs to the ground floor.

Chapter 21

The staircase, gloomy and lit only by light coming through occasional glass bricks set into the wall, was strewn with litter, rags and the bodies of flea-ridden homeless vagrants who had set up their pathetic homes on almost every landing. Tom wondered how long it took for people to notice when one of the vagrants had died. And who removed the dead body? And what did they do with it?

Minutes later, when they arrived at the second floor landing, Dalby, who was carrying the sack full of dead rats, was in the lead. He approached the bicycle and trailer which were almost blocking the landing. Tom, Dorothy, Tom's aunt and Gladwys were all following him.

'Stay away from it. Don't touch it!' said Tom sharply.

Dalby turned, startled.

Tom moved past him, turned off the switch which had operated the light above their heads, in the long since gone days when there had been a bulb in the socket, and then unfastened the end of a wire which was connected to the light socket. The other end of the wire was fixed to the metal frame of Tom's bicycle. In the gloom of the landing the wire was hardly visible. No one who didn't know it was there would have seen it.

'I see what you mean,' said Gladwys quietly. 'No one was going to steal your bicycle were they?'

'No one ever will,' said Tom firmly. 'Not if I have anything to do with it.'

Downstairs, the bodies of the two sprouts were lying on top of a stinking mixture of household rubbish. The area around the skip was littered with spilt rubbish, rotting food, unusable rags and ashes dumped from wood fires.

Tom and Dalby climbed up onto the rubbish pile and heaved out the naked bodies of the two fat sprouts. The two of them, helped by Gladwys and Dorothy then lay the bodies down in the trailer.

'What about their clothes?'

'Leave them where they are,' said Tom. 'Now the rats,' he said, nodding towards the sack that Dalby had carried down the staircase.

Dalby opened the top of the sack.

'Sprinkle them on top of the bodies,' said Tom. 'Do it so that they cover up everything human.'

'What do you usually do with these?' asked Dorothy, looking in horror as the layer of rats grew.

'I sell them,' said Dalby.

'What for?'

'As food. Usually for dogs. But sometimes for suspects who can't afford anything else. And for the skins. A woman I know skins the rats, dries the skins and uses them to make jackets. They look surprisingly good. She sells the skinned bodies to a few of her neighbours who use them to feed their dogs.'

'You can sell these when we've finished with them,' said Tom.

Dalby shrugged. 'It doesn't matter,' he said. 'There are plenty more.' He put the last few rats into the trailer.

'Take Gladwys and aunt back to our place,' Tom said to Dorothy. 'We will see you there as soon as we can.'

'Where are we taking these two?' asked Dalby, when the three women had gone. Tom had climbed onto the bicycle saddle. Dalby was walking alongside him.

Tom looked around. 'Over there,' he replied, pointing to a high rise building about half a mile away. It was as tall as the block where Dalby lived and, from a distance, looked just as dirty and uninviting. The road which connected the two was potholed and littered with the broken down, rusted remains of long abandoned vehicles. Scroungers had taken every item of possible use. There was very little motorised traffic. Anyone who needed to go somewhere travelled there on foot or by bicycle.

Chapter 22

Tom and Dalby had travelled about half the distance to the block of flats for which they were heading when a Europol security patrol, two men riding mountain bicycles, came up behind them.

'Where are you two going?' demanded the older of the two. He was in his fifties. He had a pockmarked face and lank, greasy hair poked out from underneath his peaked cap. He wore the same blue uniform as all the sprouts but, because he was a security agent, he also wore a flak jacket and had silver buttons on the cuff of his jacket sleeves. He carried a Mauser pistol in a holster on his right hip and an extendable baton on his left hip. A portable taser gun was strapped to the cross bar of his bicycle.

'Over to those flats,' said Tom.

'What for?' asked the man with the pockmarked face.

Tom pointed behind him to the rats in the trailer. 'To sell these,' he said. He looked at the two agents in turn and wondered where they came from. Traditionally, most of the Europol rank and file officers working in what had once been England came from Germany, Poland and Latvia. Recently, Tom knew, some of the newer, lower grade sprouts had been recruited from Malta and Cyprus.

The two Europol agents looked into the trailer and saw the rats piled on top of one another. They both recoiled, backed away and shuddered. 'Who buys those?' the younger one demanded.

'Lots of people buy them,' replied Dalby. 'They make good eating.' He selected a plump rat from the pile, picked it out by the tail and held it up to the Europol agent. 'Would you like this one? You can have it as a present if you like.'

The older, pockmarked security agent shuddered and shook his head. His colleague laughed. 'We eat well every night,' he boasted. 'Proper food. Fresh lamb, steak, salmon steaks.' Tom wondered if the sprout knew that Russian communism had started to collapse after Lenin had authorised a special restaurant for bureaucrats. That had been the final straw for the peasants left queuing for turnips.

'Identifications,' demanded the first agent, holding out a hand.

Tom, too wise to self-destruct, said nothing about Lenin but took out his wallet and removed his roaming licence. All suspects had to carry their roaming licences at all times. It was a serious offence not to be able to produce one when asked to do so. He handed his card to the Europol agent who scrutinised it, wrote down some details in his notebook, and then handed the card back to Tom. Dalby handed over his card and the procedure was repeated. Both Tom and Dalby still had machine readable cards but these days the Europol agents didn't carry the machines to read the cards. The Europol chiefs claimed it was part of a programme to make their agents more approachable and less mechanistic. It wasn't of course. No one in EUDCE gave a damn about approachability. The simple truth was that Europol agents didn't carry card readers solely because EUDCE couldn't get them. Most of the Europol agents didn't even have mobile telephones or two-way radios. At the end of the day the Europol agents were expected to type all the information they'd collected during the day into one of the desktop computers they still had in their offices. But most of the Europol agents were only barely literate in their own language, let alone English, and there were far too few computer keyboards for all the agents who needed them. The result, as most suspects knew, was that nothing was ever done with most of the information that was collected.

It was just bad luck that as Tom pressed down on the pedals to ride away from the two Europol agents, one of the trailer wheels caught on a piece of stone that was lying in the roadway. And it was also bad luck that the two Europol agents had not yet turned away as the trailer overturned and spilt some of its contents onto the roadway. The rats fell out first. And then one of the two naked sprout bodies half fell out onto the roadway.

'Hey!' cried the younger Europol agent, pointing to the body. 'What's that?'

The older Europol agent reacted first but he made one mistake: instead of reaching for his pistol he took out his baton. Dalby leapt at him and, before the Europol agent had managed to extend his baton, knocked him to the ground. The younger agent turned to help his colleague and so, for a moment, had his back to Tom who, without hesitation, picked up the piece of rock which had caused the accident and smashed it against the back of the sprout's head. By the time the agent had fallen to the roadway Tom had lifted the rock again and had smashed it onto the older agent's head. The older man was moving and the rock caught him a glancing blow on the neck and shoulder. But it was enough to make him cry out in pain. Before Tom could hit him again, Dalby had taken the baton and had used it to smash the sprout's skull.

The fight, if it can be called that, was over in little more than a minute.

'What the hell do we do now?' demanded Dalby, who was gasping for breath. He stood up, holding the extendable baton in his right hand and staring down at the two bodies.

'Grab their guns and batons. Empty their pockets. Make sure you take their notebooks and anything that identifies them,' said Tom, who was struggling to right the trailer. Once he'd done that he pushed the two dead sprouts who'd been in the trailer back into place and then picked up handfuls of dead rats and threw them on top. Once the layer of rats had begun to cover the bodies he spread them around, to make sure that the sprouts weren't visible.

'I'll get rid of these two,' he said to Dalby. 'Wait here.'

'Shall I take their holsters?' asked Dalby. 'What about their flak jackets?' His body was trembling with the shock of what they had done. His voice was shaking too.

'Take everything,' said Tom. 'Strip them.' He looked around. There was no one else visible for as far as he could see. The scavengers probably wouldn't come out until it was dark. Was anyone watching from one of the tower blocks? Possibly. What could they have seen? Nothing much. Tom hated snoopers just as much as he hated sprouts. Possibly more. Everywhere was grey and desolate. There were no trees, of course. They had long since been cut down to provide firewood. There was no colour. No one had money to paint privately owned buildings and EUDCE never painted anything that wasn't occupied by senior sprouts. Looking around he realised that he even missed the advertising hoardings. He'd hated them when they'd been there. Now he missed them. There were no hoardings because there was no point in advertising. Only EUDCE-approved companies had anything to sell. And they didn't need to advertise.

What on earth had happened to the world, Tom wondered. How had England come to this? He had seen pictures of Brussels and Strasbourg on the BBC. The sprouts living there enjoyed many luxuries. They had beautiful homes and office buildings, limousines and nine course meals. They flew in aeroplanes and helicopters and had their rubbish bins emptied daily. They wore soft, freshly laundered clothes every day and in the evening they sat in air-conditioned rooms where the temperature was kept at a comfortable temperature. Their electricity was provided by a mass of windmills and their supply never broke down.

'What about money?' asked Dalby. 'Should I keep their money?'

'Yes, keep the money,' said Tom.

'Where are you going?' asked Dalby, anxiously as he realised that Tom was planning to leave.

'Over there,' said Tom, nodding towards the block of flats they'd been heading for. He pressed down on the pedals. 'I'll be back as soon as I can,' he shouted over his shoulder.

Chapter 23

If there had been an Olympic speed record for riding a bicycle while towing a trailer containing two dead bodies and a good many dead rats, Tom would have broken it comfortably.

When he reached the flats he parked the bicycle and rushed up the stairs to the first floor. There wasn't time to do anything about protecting the bicycle from thieves. He just had to hope that there was no one around to try and steal it. It occurred to him too late that maybe it would have been a good idea to bring one of the guns with him. Or, maybe the taser.

The first floor of the building was deserted apart from a bundle of rags in one corner. It was impossible to see whether there was a human being amidst the rags. Tom headed for the lift doors. As with most buildings occupied by suspects, it had been a long time since the lift had worked and the doors, normally so difficult to prise apart, had been broken open years earlier. They were pulled almost together but it wasn't difficult to move them apart again. The lift itself had gone years ago. It was, thought Tom, amazing what people would and could steal. What could anyone do with a lift cabin? Take it and turn it into a home perhaps?

The empty shaft had been used as a rubbish dump and stank of rotting and decaying vegetables and animals. Tom raced back down to where his bicycle was parked. Working feverishly he threw the rats out of the trailer and then, one at a time, dragged the two bodies up the stairs to the first floor. Levering open the lift doors he half pushed and half kicked the two bodies into the lift shaft. Then he looked down. He could just make out the fact that there were two bodies down there. But maybe that was because he knew they were there. He didn't have time to cover them up. He had to get back to where Dalby was waiting. He rushed back down the stairs, threw the dead rats, or most of them, back into the trailer and then cycled back to where he had left Dalby and the two dead sprouts. Sweat was pouring from his forehead and his clothes were soaked.

'Where the hell have you been?' demanded a panicking Dalby.

He was holding one of the guns in his left hand and one of the batons in his right. 'I don't think I'm cut out for this.' The two sprouts were lying naked on the edge of the road. Their clothes were in two untidy piles.

'Stay calm,' Tom said to Dalby, although he didn't feel in the slightest bit calm himself He scooped the rats out of the trailer and threw them onto the roadway. He realised with a certain amount of horror that he no longer felt distaste at the idea of touching dead rats with his bare hands. What was happening to him? 'It's nearly over,' he said. He was exhausted; almost at his limit. 'Just help me get these two bodies into the trailer. Have you got all their ID?'

In reply Dalby put his hand into his pocket and pulled out a pile of papers.

'Good,' said Tom. 'He pulled at the first of the dead Europol agents but was so exhausted he could hardly move the body. 'Help me get these two into the trailer.' His heart was beating furiously. His fear kept him alert and watchful; it protected him. Strangely, his fear was his most powerful asset; his most effective defence.

Chapter 24

Thirty minutes later Tom and Dalby stood on the first floor, looking through the open doors and down the empty lift shaft.

The four bodies they had thrown down the lift shaft were almost invisible in the gloom. Almost but not quite. 'Go down and stay with the bicycle,' Tom told Dalby. And while Dalby guarded their valuable transport, Tom collected together armfuls of rubbish which he threw down on top of the bodies until there was nothing visible of the dead sprouts. It seemed unlikely that anyone would find them for a very long time. With any luck at all the bodies would stay until the building was demolished; at which point they would be smashed to pieces and buried under hundreds of tons of rubble.

They left the sprouts' clothes on the street half a mile away and threw the guns, the tasers and the batons down a drain a mile away. Tom used one of the batons to lever off the grating and then threw everything down into the water below.

'Shouldn't we keep these?' asked Dalby as Tom tossed away the weapons.

'Tempting,' agreed Tom. He paused, holding the last gun. 'But just too risky.' He dropped it, listened for the splash and then he put back the grating.

He tore the identity papers into pieces and threw them down another drain. They shared the money they had taken. It wasn't much but it was more than they'd seen for a long, long time.

And then it began to rain: a torrential, monsoon type storm.

Even old-fashioned English weather seemed to have disappeared, along with cricket, crumpets and other manifestations of the old-fashioned English way of life.

This was no shower, not even a rainstorm. The rain came down so fast and so heavily that they were soaked to the skin within seconds.

But somehow it didn't seem to matter.

Chapter 25

Several hours later, after a bath in hot water (a rare treat in a world where such a luxury could cost as much as a man's suit but was something of a necessity when a man has been handling human bodies, dead rats and armfuls of garbage all day long) and an extravagant meal of roast potatoes and raw carrots, Tom and Dorothy sat together in their tiny living room.

The potatoes and the carrots had come from the allotment where Tom worked. They were gifts from allotment holders. Most of the people who had allotments grew high production crops – such as beans. Carrots, which were difficult to produce in the exhausted soil, were rare. Tom and Dorothy usually ate the carrots raw to ensure that they got as much of the vitamin content as possible.

'One of the gardeners at the allotment has some tomato plants growing,' said Tom. 'If they produce any fruit he's promised to give me two – one for each of us.' If it ever happened it would be a highlight.

Dorothy had lit the wood burning stove and had opened the doors so that they could enjoy the sight of the flames inside. They opened a small bar of fruit and nut chocolate which Dorothy had been given by a grateful client. It was three years past its 'best before' date. The chocolate may have tasted a trifle stale but it was such a long time since they'd tasted anything like it that their taste buds had nothing with which to compare it.

Tom's aunt was asleep in her room and they carefully wrapped her share of the chocolate back in its paper. Dalby and Gladwys, reassured and now too tired (both mentally and physically) to worry overmuch, were in their 16th floor flat.

Tom and Dorothy sipped sherry. It wasn't a drink either of them was particularly fond of but it was slightly more palatable than potato wine. And Dalby had bought two bottles with some of the money he had taken from the Europol agents. One bottle for each couple.

'You OK?' asked Dorothy.

Tom nodded, stretched his legs and grunted. The fire crackled and spat a little.

'Four more,' said Dorothy.

'Four more,' agreed Tom. 'Six dead sprouts.' He had never felt so tired. But he didn't want to go to bed.

There was a long silence. They both watched the flames flickering in the log burning stove.

'Taking the money doesn't seem right.'

'It worries me more than the killing,' said Tom. 'But it's daft to worry about it. They're dead. The money would have just gone into the lift shaft if we hadn't taken it. We need it.'

'We can certainly use it.'

They watched the flames for a while.

'I love real fires,' said Tom. The fire was a necessity but it was, strangely, also one of their few luxuries.

'Me too.'

They sat and watched but said nothing.

'Gladwys said she has three friends who are in the same boat as they were,' said Dorothy at last.

Tom looked across at her.

'About to have to share their home with strangers.'

'And she knows one couple who are being deported for not paying their Telescreen licence. They'll be sent to Africa to work on the grain farms.'

'There's a lot of injustice out there.'

'And a lot of anger.'

They sat and sipped their sherry.

'It's a pity Dalby couldn't get whisky,' said Tom.

'Yes. Sherry is a very strange drink isn't it. It seems like alcohol but...' Dorothy didn't finish the sentence.

'It's a big but.'

'Are we going to stop now?'

'Stop what?'

'Stop killing sprouts.'

'You want to kill some more?'

'It's the only way we can do anything to change things. Voting doesn't make any difference. Protesting in the streets doesn't make any difference...'

'...and gets you arrested or beaten to death.'

'There's a lot of justifiable rage out there. A lot of people are very angry. A lot of people want to do something.'

'Maybe they just like whingeing. Maybe they'll moan but not do anything.'

'Gladwys says she thinks people are ready to stand up and do something. We talked while you and Dalby were out.'

'Ready to stand up and kill sprouts?'

'She says she thinks they are.'

'What do you think?'

'I don't know. But I do know that we don't have much choice. Do you want to carry on as things are?'

'No. No, I don't want to just carry on as things are. But do you really think killing sprouts will change anything?'

'It might do. It would certainly help keep people sane. It would give people hope. Something positive to do and to fight for.'

'Then perhaps we'd better organise a meeting.'

'That's what Gladwys and I thought.'

'Oh you did, did you?'

'We did. Would you like another glass of sherry?'

'Why not? It's better than potato wine. And I feel like getting tiddly.'

'Do you think we can get tiddly on sherry?'

'I don't have the foggiest. Let's find out.'

Tom picked up the bottle and refilled their glasses.

'Where are we going to hold this meeting?'

'Not here.'

'No, of course not.'

'So, where?'

'I'll think of somewhere. But we need to do some serious thinking before we have a meeting.'

'What about?'

'Well, for a start we need to find a better way to get rid of the bodies. We can't go on tossing them down lift shafts or leaving them in hospital corridors.'

'Someone might see us?'

'Someone might see us,' agreed Dorothy. 'And eventually, someone is going to start finding the bodies. Then even the Europol idiots might begin to suspect that something is going on.'

'So we need to work out how we can get rid of the bodies. Killing them isn't difficult, but hiding the bodies is a problem.'

'Killing them could get more difficult.'

'Why?'

'So far, the sprouts haven't expected to be hit on the head and so it's been easy to take them by surprise. But we can't rely on that for ever. Once it becomes known that sprouts are being killed they'll all get edgy. Even ordinary sprouts will start carrying weapons.'

'That's another reason for hiding the bodies so that they aren't found. If there aren't any bodies lying around then the authorities may just suspect that the missing sprouts have gone AWOL. They won't want to start claiming that sprouts are being murdered when they haven't even got any bodies. They'd look silly.'

Dorothy thought about this. 'You're right. We have to find some way to get rid of the bodies without anyone finding them.'

'I need more thinking juice.'

'Thinking juice?'

'Sherry.'

'Ah. OK. I thought you didn't like this stuff?'

'It's growing on me. Every glass I drink tastes better than the previous one.'

Chapter 26

Sitting back in her reclining leather chair (designed for captains of ships and industry and retailing at a sumptuous 3,000 euros including all taxes) Chief Commissioner Dame Phyllis Stein, Provincial Commissioner for Administration and Protector of the People for Province 17 (formerly known as the United Kingdom and now subdivided into 12 subregions, each with its own Regional Parliament and Regional Commissioner), glowered at the sprout sitting in front of her (on a far less luxurious chair).

Born in Poland but now loyal to her new homeland, the United States of Europe, Chief Commissioner Stein wore her hair short, as short as a private soldier in the English army of the 1950's, a haircut that used to be known as a 'short back and sides', and was dressed in a heavy-weight wool trouser suit in a chalk stripe with a matching five button waistcoat and a Royal Engineers tie (which she wore because she thought it looked masculine and clubbish). She wore no make-up, not even lipstick or anything to disguise her rather grey, deathly pallor, and she wore no jewellery of any kind. The mannish effect she sought was rather spoilt by her bathukolpian figure which made her look what she was: a short-haired, butch lesbian wearing the sort of suit a man might wear.

She was variously described by those around her as arrogant, conceited and concerned only with her own pleasures and extravagances. It would have been difficult to find anyone prepared to disagree with these judgements in private though no one, of course, would have agreed with them in public. Her enemies thought of her less kindly than this.

Within the Region the Chief Commissioner possessed the sort of power over the English that would have last been enjoyed by a Roman consul. She enjoyed, in the true sense of the word, a considerable reputation for ruthlessness and she ran her region as though it were her personal property. When, during a particularly cold winter spell, an aide had suggested releasing some supplies of logs for junior sprouts and suspects she had cackled with laughter, demoted him two grades (an almost unheard of event) and transferred him to Glasgow. She told everyone she saw that the aide had been having what she called 'a transient human experience'.

Under her supervision, and with her authority, profligacy and waste had become a purpose instead of an irritating consequence of inattention. (If a man bakes bread every day of his working life then it is reasonable to describe him as a baker; baking bread is what he does. Similarly, if a government wastes money efficiently and with regularity it becomes difficult to argue with the thesis that the primary purpose of the government is just that: to waste money.)

Although EUDCE had done its best to rid England of most of its history, and had done so with remarkable, custom-crushing efficiency, it had embraced one glorious part of Olde England: the traditional honours system.

The honours systems in much of Europe had been dismantled generations earlier, but the bureaucratic aristocrats who now ran EUDCE rather enjoyed the idea of decorating themselves, and adding the extra dignity to which they felt they were entitled, by making themselves Sirs, Dames, Ladies and Lords. And so, since there was nothing and no one to stop them, that's exactly what they did.

***

Dame Phyllis was moaning because one of her Deputy Chief Assistant Commissioners, Israeli-born Sir Czardas Tsastske, had just confessed that neither he nor anyone else working in the Regional Offices could tell her how many suspects were now living in the Region.

Sir Czardas had been born Percival Liebermann but had changed his name to something which he thought would offer him a better chance of rising high within the EUDCE hierarchy. Many of EUDCE's high-ranking security officers had been born in Israel, the last nation to join the European Union before it morphed painlessly into EUDCE, but most of them had adopted names which might have once been more widely found in the telephone directories of the countries formerly known as belonging to Eastern Europe.

Sir Czardas had made a personal fortune selling confiscated penknives in the first decade of the 21st century. ('Well, what did you think we were going to do with them?' he demanded of an indignant purchaser who had bought back his own multi-bladed Swiss Army penknife; a snip at two thirds of the original cost.)

'It's so much more difficult to keep track of people when they're not employed by us,' explained Sir Czardas Tsastske. He was considerably shorter than he would have liked to have been and plumper than was good for him but he had long ago decided that since he could do nothing about the former he would do nothing about the latter. He enjoyed food and had managed to convince himself that longevity (and its antithesis) are consequences of inheritance rather than appetite. His parents had died in a car crash and he had convinced himself that without that intervention they would have lived into their 90's, if not beyond.

He had very little hair and that which he had, and which was visible to the casual observer, was largely situated in and around his ears. He dressed formally, in three piece pin-striped suits which he had made by a Chinese tailor in Savile Row, but allowed his flamboyant nature to express itself with the aid of flashy silk ties and handkerchiefs which he purchased in bulk from a small haberdashery store in the Burlington Arcade. Both the tailor and the haberdasher had originally catered for the old English aristocracy. These days they catered for the new European aristocracy. No one other than EUDCE employees could afford their prices, which were at the obscene end of absurd.

'When they're properly employed they're frightened of losing their jobs. They're so much easier to control. As things are now it's becoming easier to control the sprouts than the damned moutons.' (Like many senior sprouts he invariably referred to suspects as 'moutons'.)

He glanced at the huge Telescreen, always switched on, which was fixed to the wall directly above the Chief Commissioner's head. A matching Telescreen dominated the wall behind him. The screens were positioned so that both the Chief Commissioner and her visitor could keep up with everything that was going on. Every EUDCE employee, even those with senior positions, were terrified of missing something, anything, that they might be expected to have seen.

On the screen a tall woman with a tattooed scalp, who had failed at several careers and had consequently become a highly successful fashion model, news reader and Telescreen personality, was interviewing two raggedy young beggars standing outside a railway station in Bucharest.

The woman beggar, dressed in a micro skirt and a very skimpy top, carried a baby in her arms. The man, dressed inexplicably in a top hat and tails, had a dog curled up at his feet. The beggars, both English, were explaining that they'd travelled to Romania because a careers advisor had assured them that there were more opportunities for beggars there.

'For a while we sold copies of a magazine called La Grande Question,' explained the woman. 'But then we attended a begging school run by two experienced Romanians and they told us we could make more money without it.'

'Is it a boy or a girl?' asked the interviewer, smiling at the baby and making goo goo noises.

'I dunno,' said the girl. 'It's not ours.'

'Not yours? Are you looking after it for someone?'

'We rent it,' said the girl. 'Monday, Wednesday and Friday mornings.'

The interviewer seemed surprised.

'We'd like to have it Saturdays,' said the girl. 'But there's a waiting list for Saturdays. And by the time we get to the top of the waiting list the baby will be too old. So we're trying to get on another waiting list.'

'We have a little handwritten note in eight languages,' said her boyfriend, a lanky Scottish youth. He showed a scruffy piece of paper to the interviewer.

'What does it say?'

'It says we're poor and starving and the baby is sick and needs antibiotics,' said the boy.

'Is that true?'

The boy looked at her, as though trying to decide whether she was naive or stupid or both, and frowned.

'Is the dog yours or is that rented?' asked the interviewer.

'Why would we rent a dog?' asked the boy, as though only a stupid person would ask such a question. 'Renting dogs doesn't make commercial sense. You can pick 'em up in the street for nothing.'

The Chief Commissioner, who had watched this exchange without emotion, turned away from the Telescreen. 'I hear another twenty two sprouts have disappeared.' She paused and looked over the top of a pair of imaginary spectacles at Sir Czardas. She believed this gave her a rather academic air. 'How can sprouts just disappear?' she demanded. 'Where do they go to? Have they absconded? Been kidnapped?' She picked up a diecast model of a 1931 Alfa Romeo which she kept on her desk. It was too pristine to have ever been played with by a careless child.

Sir Czardas looked uncomfortable. 'I think these are just rumours,' he said.

'So what do you think is going on?' demanded the Chief Commissioner. 'I really need to get my ducks in a row on this one.'

'Maybe people are trying to claim pensions for sprouts who didn't exist?' suggested Sir Czardas.

'Would anyone do that?' asked the Chief Commissioner frowning. 'Isn't that cheating?'

'I'm afraid it is and they might,' said Sir Czardas.

'It comes to a fine thing when the people start cheating the system,' said the Chief Commissioner who firmly believed that in a decent world things should happen the other way round. She sighed, genuinely disappointed. 'I sometimes think we may be losing touch with our subjects,' she said. 'Wrongsiding the demographic.' She paused and thought. 'We need to do something to make the people feel proud,' she said, as pleased with this thought as a mathematician might have been if he'd just found a flaw in something Einstein had written. 'Something grand. Sprinkle a little magic.'

Sir Czardas had noticed the use of the word 'subjects'. But he said nothing. He was by no means the first person to realise that you don't get to be a senior regulator within the EUDCE hierarchy by noticing things that you weren't intended to notice.

The Chief Commissioner watched with mild dismay as two bare knuckled fighters circled each other on the Telescreen. It was the weekly *Fight to the Death*. The winner received a small pension and a book of food stamps. The loser didn't get anything but since it was a fight to the death he wouldn't need anything. It had long ago occurred to her that the people who appeared on these programmes would do almost anything to appear on the Telescreen. She wondered, indeed, if there was a limit. Was there anything any of them wouldn't do? She remembered reading that towards the end of the 20th century a majority of Olympic athletes had agreed that they would take drugs that improved their performance, and increased their chances of winning a medal, even if doing so meant that they would die within a few years because of the side effects. And then she remembered another piece of research which had shown that, when invited to choose between 'the Telescreen' and 'daddy', a majority of small children had chosen the Telescreen. She didn't quite know what any of this proved and, indeed, couldn't be bothered to work out if it meant anything. But she thought it probably all meant something and helped explain what was happening.

On the Telescreen one of the men was gouging at the other's eyes with his fingers. She turned her head and her gaze was attracted to a print of a painting of EUDCE's Brussels headquarters. It was a standard print, issued to all senior sprouts throughout the EUDCE region. She loathed the picture and looked away quickly. It was a hideous building and a hideous painting. The Chief Commissioner collected art and had grown to believe that she had quite an eye. She was in the fortunate position that no one was likely to disagree with this belief. Her office contained two beautiful Abbotsford chairs ('for looking at not sitting on' she once told a visitor who had made the mistake of dropping her ample bottom onto the delicate seat), an early Georgian bookcase (which contained the Chief Commissioner's collection of model soldiers) an early Regency chest of drawers and a Carolean day bed which had once graced the hallway in one of England's stately homes. She had been enormously flattered when a former Professor of Art History, who had specialised in English furniture and who had been employed as a chauffeur at the Regional Parliament, had swallowed his pride and described her collection as 'eclectic'. She had promoted the former academic and put him in charge of the mailroom. It was an undemanding job since the takeover of the postal services of Europe by EUDCE meant that correspondence that didn't travel by fax, e-mail or courier usually didn't travel very far at all. Having him in the building meant that if she ever wanted to ask his advice she could do so without delay. She had not yet asked his advice, though she had on numerous occasions invited his approval. He had learned to keep his opinions to himself but to offer enthusiastic approbation without hesitation.

Her favourite piece in the room was the sculpture she'd bought some years earlier and which now stood on a windowsill. It was a bust of a woman who had shoulder length hair a high, proud forehead and a perfect, aquiline nose. The sculptor had completed the bust by capturing the beginnings of an impressive embonpoint.

The Chief Commissioner was not a woman who allowed her emotions to affect her life in any serious way ('emotions are for books' was her favourite saying, though she herself never read anything that didn't have an index and a long list of references at the back) but she had fallen in love with the bust, which she thought was very fine art.

'Have they mended my Bentley?' she asked suddenly. Apart from her art collection, the Chief Commissioner's main interest was her extensive collection of motor cars. She had twelve, including a Ferrari, a Lamborghini, a Rolls Royce, two BMWs and a 1955 Bentley S1. Unfortunately, the Chief Commissioner, who enjoyed driving, always expected other motorists to get out of her way (she flew a small flag on whichever car she was using to make it clear who was inside) and she sometimes overestimated the ability of other drivers to do this expeditiously. The Bentley, painted black and with blacked out windows, had been damaged in a collision with a small delivery vehicle.

Sir Czardas coughed nervously. 'I understand there's some problem with finding a replacement headlamp glass,' he said. He wiped sweat off his forehead and upper lip. Generally speaking it was not, he knew, a good idea to disappoint the Chief Commissioner. The Chief Commissioner grunted to show her dissatisfaction. 'I need it mended quickly,' she said. She always used the word 'need' in preference to 'want'. 'It's a family heirloom.' The Bentley hadn't belonged to her family, her family hadn't owned anything grander than a bucket, but it had been someone else's family heirloom and that, she thought, entitled her to describe it as a family heirloom. She looked again at the bust on the windowsill. Looking at it always soothed her. She found it quietly inspirational. 'What we need is something to lift the people.' She thought of all the people (sprouts and suspects) as 'her people'. Her subjects.

'What a marvellous idea,' said Sir Czardas, nodding like one of those dogs motorists used to put on the back shelf in their cars. 'Brilliant!'

On the Telescreen a new programme had started. Programmes on the Telescreen were as short as attention spans. A tall, weedy, dark-skinned youth in a powder blue suit and a floppy yellow bowtie was introducing the BBC's daily Clip from China, a fifteen minute programme broadcast on the instructions of the Commissariat in Brussels in order to improve relations between EUDCE and China, and to extend understanding of the Chinese people among the citizens of the United States of Europe.

'We need to find some way of commemorating the great work of the leaders of the European Superstate,' said the Chief Commissioner. 'A new memorial for EUDCE. A celebration of our coming legacy. A remembrance of the great work done here. A grand memento that will leverage inspiration for the people for generations to come.'

'That would be tremendously invigorating,' agreed Sir Czardas. 'Everyone would be enthused.'

'Enthusing the people is what I do best,' said the Chief Commissioner who was so out of touch that she genuinely believed this. She picked up a Mont Blanc pen and fiddled with it. Modesty, she believed, was either an affectation, to be despised, or an honest admission of mediocrity.

'A wall plaque perhaps?' suggested Sir Czardas, who always thought small. 'A nice plaque fitted inside the entrance hall. You could unveil it a week on Saturday.' He drew back a pair of small, imaginary curtains. 'We could have your name inscribed on a nice oblong made of genuine plastic.'

'Oh no,' said the Chief Commissioner, shaking her head. 'We need something much grander than that. Remember the Night Watch, that magnificent painting by whatshisname which commemorated those...' she waved a hand, indicating that whoever they were they weren't worth her struggling to remember. 'Those people,' she finished, rather lamely.

'The painting hanging in the EUDCE President's outer office?' suggested Sir Czardas. 'I think you will find it was by the Dutch painter, Rembrandt. He was commissioned to paint a Dutch Captain and a number of his militia men.'

'That's the one,' agreed the Chief Commissioner who didn't much like people showing that they knew more than she did. 'Something like that but larger maybe. Or perhaps we could build a new Taj Mahal. It's about time the world had an eighth wonder.' She paused, her face flushed with excitement. 'Would you like some afternoon tea?'

'That would be very nice,' agreed Sir Czardas. The sprouts all lived well (even the lower grade officials enjoyed a more than comfortable standard of living) but the Chief Commissioner lived particularly well. Her afternoon teas were legendary.

The Chief Commissioner pressed a button on the intercom on her desk, spoke to Clothilde, her personal assistant, a pretty young sprout in her early twenties who had no discernible secretarial skills but always wore very short black skirts and revealing, diaphanous white blouses which just happened to be a uniform the Chief Commissioner favoured, and ordered tea for two. She turned back to the Telescreen. 'What's that?' she asked.

The young man in the blue suit was standing in front of what looked like a massive army of soldiers standing to attention. 'I'm standing in the mausoleum of the First Qin Emperor of China which dates from 210 BC,' the young man murmured in that quiet, reverential way that presenters have always favoured when reporting on royal funerals or when broadcasting from churches, museums and European Parliament buildings. 'Behind me stands the terracotta army, an astonishing 8,000 individual figures, mainly soldiers, but also acrobats, musicians, strongmen and horse drawn chariots. Every member of this army stands around two metres tall and the whole creation was built as a tribute, a glorification, a great memorial.'

'That's it!' murmured the Chief Commissioner.

Sir Czardas looked at her.

'The sculptors used eight basic face moulds and then used clay to create the soldiers' facial expressions,' continued the thin man in the blue suit.

There was a polite knock on the door.

'Come!' called the Chief Commissioner.

The Chief Commissioner's personal assistant entered pushing a beautifully hand-carved oak tea trolley. On the top level of the trolley stood a solid silver tea pot, a solid silver sugar bowl with solid silver sugar tongs, a solid silver milk creamer (in the shape of a cow), a solid silver water jug, a solid silver tea strainer, solid silver cutlery and two cups, two saucers and two plates, all in rare 19th century Meissen porcelain. On the lower level of the trolley there were two three-tiered stands, each consisting of three plates connected by a silver rod and a single, larger Meissen plate. One set of tiered plates contained small triangular sandwiches with the crusts cut off and the other contained small fancy cakes. The single plate contained a large, uncut sponge cake and a solid silver cake knife.

'The English used to have bread and butter at teatime,' said the Chief Commissioner, as the personal assistant lifted the items off the trolley and placed them on the Chief Commissioner's desk. 'I never understood that,' she said. 'Why eat bread and butter when you could be eating cake?'

'I think that is perhaps why the English are extinct,' said Sir Czardas. 'Their self-restraint eventually proved to be destructive.'

The Chief Commissioner thought about this for a moment, pursed her lips and then nodded. 'You could be right.'

'Will there be anything else you will be requiring?' asked Clothilde, the personal assistant. She was from Estonia and spoke English with a very thick accent which the Chief Commissioner found most appealing. This was one of the few phrases she knew and she always managed to endow it with more meaning than might normally be expected. The Chief Commissioner, knowing that the personal assistant wouldn't understand anything she said in reply, just smiled and waved her away.

'Statues,' said the Chief Commissioner with the great certainty of one who knows that her audience will agree wholeheartedly with whatever she says. 'We will have our own statues made to celebrate EUDCE,' she continued, having paused to watch the girl leave, and to enjoy the view. If she'd been alone she would have accidentally-on-purpose dropped a spoon so that she could tell the girl to pick it up. 'They will be an ever-growing monument to our new State's continuing and ever growing glory. A glorious tribute to the State's munificence.'

'Brilliant,' said Sir Czardas, who would have enthused if the Chief Commissioner had suggested building a full-scale model of the Eiffel Tower out of oyster shells.

'And I know just the person to create the sculptures for us!' said the Chief Commissioner. She pointed at the bust of the young woman which stood on her windowsill. 'Find the sculptor who created that bust,' she said. 'Put her in charge of the project.'

'Do you know the sculptor?' asked Sir Czardas.

'I'm sure the bust must have been made by a woman,' said the Chief Commissioner. 'No man could have made something so beautiful.'

'How will we find the name of the sculptor?' asked Sir Czardas, nervously.

'Lift it up,' said the Chief Commissioner. 'I seem to remember that there was something scratched on the underside.' Sir Czardas stood up and moved across to the windowsill.

'But be careful with it,' warned the Chief Commissioner. 'If you drop it I'll have you posted to Scotland.' She laughed lightly and selected a cucumber sandwich. 'When you've done that you can be mother and pour the tea,' she said, putting the sandwich whole into her mouth. Sir Czardas didn't want to be posted to Scotland. Just that morning there had been yet another outbreak of rioting in Ville 723 (the town formerly known as Glasgow). Another group of Scottish nationalists had belatedly realised that their Parliament (the one they thought was a proper parliament and the first step to independence) was really just a EUDCE regional parliament and that their hopes of independence were now further away than they had been since the Union with England had been formally approved. When EUDCE had officially broken up Great Britain the Scottish nationalists had cheered and waved their saltire flags for days. It was taking some of them years to realise just how much they had been betrayed by the people they'd welcomed as saviours.

'Certainly, ma'am,' said Sir Czardas, who secretly adored strong women and fantasised that one day the Chief Commissioner would command him to clean her shoes with his tongue. He found the name on the bottom of the bust, and made a note of it in a small notebook with a silver pencil. He turned, just before he left. 'And do you want me to do anything about the missing sprouts?'

'Nothing,' replied the Chief Commissioner, now clearly irritated by the question and the whole idea of missing sprouts. 'They've probably taken unauthorised leave. Some of these people have no sense of loyalty or responsibility but we don't want to advertise that fact. If we make a fuss we'll upset people. We'll demoralise the sprouts, who will worry, and the suspects will be concerned because some of their betters have gone missing.' She gazed at the bust, which Sir Czardas had put back on the windowsill. She didn't think he'd put it back in quite the right position. 'And can you imagine the damage that would be done to our bonuses if people in Brussels thought that we were running such an unhappy ship that sprouts were actually leaving their posts?'

'You don't think they could have been...?' Sir Czardas's voice fell. He suddenly realised that he shouldn't have started the question. The Chief Commissioner's eyes seemed to bore right through him. He closed his eyes for a moment.

'...could have been what?' demanded the Chief Commissioner.

'Er...killed? Murdered?'

'Don't be silly,' snapped the Chief Commissioner. 'Who would murder them? Sprouts aren't going to kill sprouts. And suspects wouldn't dare. And even if they did dare what would they do with the bodies? We control all the mortuaries and the cemeteries.'

'There were those two bodies at the hospital,' said Sir Czardas.

'A road accident,' said the Chief Commissioner with a wave of a hand. She pointed to the bust on her windowsill. 'Just find the sculptor who made that bust,' snapped the Chief Commissioner. 'That's what I want you to do.' She nibbled at a sandwich. 'And loop back to me just as soon as you've found her.'

She waited until Sir Czardas had gone and then stood up, moved to the windowsill and corrected the position of the bust a few millimetres. If you wanted something doing you really had to do it your self

Chapter 27

For the first couple of days Tom and Dorothy and Dalby and Gladwys waited for something to happen; for the sky to fall in, the earth to swallow them up. (Tom's aunt had no fears, any more than she had expectations, ambitions or hopes. She lived for now, in a private world of the present, where time meant nothing.) If the sprouts had burst through their doors, they would have stood there unprotesting, waiting to be shot.

But, as the days went by, so they came to think that perhaps there would be no sudden bursting of the door lock under the weight of an enthusiastically wielded battering ram. (The security forces never knocked.)

And nothing happened.

There were no raids. No armed sprouts burst through their doors firing machine guns. There was no nerve gas sprayed through the windows. None of the 'kill first, make up explanations later' that had become official policy since the long ago days when the police had got away with shooting a tube train passenger in cold blood, and had realised that they could do exactly what they wanted and get away with it. (The police had discovered that without the sort of platform for dissent offered by a free press or an unregulated Internet – both of which were, thanks to EUDCE's Strategic Freedoms Policy no more than distant memories – there was nothing for them to fear from using what they called 'preventive techniques' to control potential or suspected terrorists. 'A well-shot suspect fires no guns and makes no complaints' was a favourite maxim among Europol officers.)

The five of them and the cat met the following Saturday in a nearby park. They chose a spot near the lake where they could look out over the water towards a small island. There had been benches there but they had long gone; chopped up by people looking for wood to burn. Pieces of metal from the benches lay around, discarded and unwanted. The park was now almost empty of trees and the larger bushes had all gone; taken for burning. Even the island was bare of trees and bushes. Only grass and weeds grew there now, though some of the weeds were five or six feet high. Within the main part of the park the grass had spread over what had once been beautiful ornamental flowerbeds. Only the paths, wide ribbons of tarmacadam, now decorated with bunches of grass and weed which had broken through the surface, remained of the original park.

There was a small exception.

There was one small part of the park that remained as it had once been; a small section that could be seen from offices belonging to senior sprouts.

Three gardeners, all suspects, worked on this small segment of garden to keep it looking smart and pretty. The area was fenced off so that other suspects couldn't walk on the paths, see the flowers or interfere with the view from the sprouts' offices.

In the old days there had been ducks and swans on the lake. Tom had often stopped to feed the birds pieces of bread as he'd strolled through the park, especially on cold winter days when there was little for them to eat. Occasionally, there had been young mothers with small children, cosy in thick coats, scarves and hats, holding bags full of pieces of torn up bread, standing by the waterside. But there had been no waterfowl in the park for a long time. They had long since been caught, cooked and eaten. Even the pigeons in the park had gone. All killed and eaten. Only the occasional hardy, sparrow remained; ever nervous, ever watchful. Alive only because the meat on a sparrow isn't worth the catching. You'd use up more energy catching one than you'd obtain by eating one.

'Do you think we got away with it?' whispered Gladwys. Even sitting in the park she was nervous. She had good reason to be. The BBC had, that morning, broadcast news that a group of 500 suspects who had been accused of Respect Deficit had been deported to Africa to work on one of Monsanto-Goldman-Sach's EUDCE croplands. The suspects were shown boarding the converted tanker that would take them on their one-way journey. The newsreader had described, with undisguised relish, the terrible conditions on the vessel and the equally bad conditions which awaited the deportees when they arrived at their destination. (Respect Deficit was a common charge. Any sprout who felt that he had not been treated with sufficient respect could make the charge. It was well-known that whenever the farms needed more labourers the sprouts would be encouraged to bring charges if a suspect so much as failed to lower his eyes when spoken to.)

'I think so,' said Tom.

The four of them stood in silence for a while, staring at the lake. The water was thick and sludgy and it stank. Tom's aunt had wandered off and, together with Tabatha, was watching one of the lonely sparrows.

'So,' said Dalby. 'What do we do now?'

'Two choices,' said Tom. 'First choice: we retire while we're ahead. Think ourselves lucky and keep our heads down.'

'And hope the sprouts leave us alone,' said Dalby.

'And hope the sprouts leave us alone,' agreed Dorothy.

'Which they won't,' sighed Dalby.

'Which they certainly will not,' agreed Dorothy.

'Or?' said Gladwys.

'Second choice: we decide that we're not going to let the sprouts continue to bully us and run our lives.'

'Does that mean what I suspect it means?' asked Gladwys. 'That we prepare to kill some more sprouts when they cause us trouble?'

'More than that,' said Tom. 'That's more of a halfway house. Call it the second option. And if that's the second option then there's a third option.'

The others looked at him.

'We kill sprouts who are causing other people trouble.'

'A sort of revolution,' said Dalby.

Tom nodded. 'A sort of revolution.'

They looked out at the stinking lake and for a while no one spoke.

'This used to be beautiful,' said Gladwys at last. 'I used to come here all the time. I remember there were fish in the water. The water was so clear you could see them swimming around.'

'We were lucky with those six,' said Dalby. 'No one saw us kill them. No one saw us get rid of the bodies. No one seemed to notice that six sprouts were missing. I can't help feeling that killing more is going to be dangerous.'

'I don't care if it is dangerous,' said Dorothy. 'I don't know about the rest of you but I don't honestly feel I have all that much to lose. It's not been much of a life recently.'

The other three thought about this for a while. But it wasn't a point of view with which they felt able to disagree.

'You have to have something to believe in,' said Tom. 'This has given me a new lease of life. I want to kill as many of them as possible. Ridding the world of the vermin.'

'But won't the Commissioners simply recruit more?' asked Gladwys.

'If your kitchen is infested with cockroaches do you leave them and say there is no point in killing them because more will come, or do you try and wipe them out?'

'So, what do we do now?' asked Dalby.

'If we want to start a revolution we need more people,' said Tom. 'We can't make a real difference by ourselves. You can't start a revolution with four people.'

'Five if we count your aunt,' said Dorothy, pointing at Tom's aunt.

'Five,' agreed Tom. His aunt had found a large branch in the thick weeds. The branch was bigger than she was but she was dragging it back towards them so that they could take it home for firewood.

'We need to find people who think the way we do...' began Gladwys.

'...that's everyone!' interrupted Dalby. 'All the suspects.'

'...yes, I agree,' continued Gladwys. 'But we need to find people who think the way we do and are prepared to do something; prepared to stand up and try to make a difference.' She looked at Dalby. 'And that's *not* everyone!'

'No, you're right,' Dalby agreed. 'We need a revolutionary army!'

The others looked at him.

'Sort of thing,' he said, suddenly embarrassed.

'We can't have an old-fashioned revolution.'

'No. They've got too many guns.'

'We have to kill them one at a time.'

There was a pause and a long silence.

'How long do you think it would take?'

'We've got nothing else to do.'

'How many people do you think we could get together?'

Dalby and Gladwys looked at each other, murmuring possible names. Tom and Dorothy did the same.

'We know a dozen, maybe 15,' said Dalby.

'We can probably manage something near to that,' said Tom.

'We need somewhere to meet,' said Dorothy. 'We can't have that many people in one of our homes.'

'And we can't meet outside in the street,' said Dalby. 'What about an empty shop or an old warehouse? There are plenty of those around?'

'They're all known to the sprouts and they're all under surveillance,' said Tom.

'We need a building which is guaranteed to be empty at night and which won't be under constant surveillance,' said Dorothy, thoughtfully. 'Somewhere which we know won't be bugged.'

'Sproutland!' said Tom's aunt.

They all looked at her.

'The sprout buildings don't have cameras in them,' she said.

'She's right!' said Tom. He put his arm around his aunt, pulled her to him and gave her a big kiss on the cheek. 'The police station closes at 5 p.m. They don't have any cameras inside. They took them all out after the fuss that was made when a group of suspects were beaten to death.' The inquiry into the revelations of police brutality had recommended that all CCTV cameras be removed from the police stations to protect the privacy of serving police officers.

'But they might have bugs,' said Dalby. 'I can think of somewhere even better!'

'Where?'

'The Regional Parliament,' said Dalby. 'The buildings all close at 5 p.m. and shut at weekends. No one ever works there in the evenings.'

'I bet they're warm too!' said Gladwys.

'Can we get in?' asked Dalby. 'Don't they have tons of security?'

'I doubt it,' said Dorothy. 'How many people want to break into the Regional Parliament building?'

Chapter 28

Tom and Dalby broke into the building the following evening. It was astonishingly easy.

The Regional Parliament building had been built several decades earlier, but had been kept a secret for many years. There was no little irony in the fact that at the same time as ordinary citizens were losing their right to privacy so the State was constantly shrouding everything it did in layers of secrecy and deceit. EUDCE had reversed the natural order of things. Once, everything individuals did was their business, and their business alone, while everything their government did on their behalf was public business. The rise and rise of the European Union, and EUDCE, had turned things upside down, inside out and back to front.

Politicians at the House of Commons had kept quiet about the unelected Regional Parliaments, which had been built, under instructions from what had then been known as the European Union. They had, of course, all been part of the plan to replace the United Kingdom in general, and England in particular, with a series of political regions. The Parliaments had, like everything else prepared for the European Union, been built without consideration for cost. European Regional Parliamentary buildings in Scotland, Wales, Northern Ireland and London had, one by one, and with a great fanfare of publicity, been opened as examples of just how the central Government was giving back power to the people. Few had realised that these Parliaments were merely a physical manifestation of power moving not towards the regions, and towards the people, but towards Brussels and towards the bureaucrats. Few had realised that London would soon be renamed Ville 4178.

The European Union had found it remarkably easy to take over the United Kingdom. Under the guidance of home-grown politicians who had been bribed and flattered into submission, the nation had lain back and abandoned itself to defeat and total domination without a gun being fired. The nation which had conquered the world and ruled an empire had disappeared and been replaced by a series of anonymous regions. Cromwell's Parliament, which had shown the model for parliaments elsewhere, had, knowingly and apparently with enthusiasm, and the approval of a trusting monarch, committed suicide. The Parliament where Churchill had argued and fought was now empty and silent. The nation, and the monarchy, for which millions had lain down their lives, was now merely a small and insignificant part of the new European Superstate.

It was easy to break into the building because no one working for the European Superstate imagined for one moment that anyone would break in. Why would they? There was nothing much to steal. There were no secrets to take. The Regional Parliaments were merely local rubber stamps for the European Commission, the powerhouse of Europe, and that edentulous homage to democracy, the European Parliament.

They got in through a fire door that had been left open by staff members who, judging by the number of cigarette butts on the ground nearby, used the doorway and the shelter provided by the small canopy over it, as somewhere to stand when taking their smoking breaks.

For many years EUDCE had had a double-edged approach to smoking; it had two official policies. On the one hand EUDCE's first, and best known, official policy was to discourage smoking. In the old Europe, smoking had killed more people than the two World Wars of the 20th century. EUDCE had introduced a good deal of legislation designed to attack this problem.

But the other official policy was to encourage tobacco farmers. Over the years, countless billions of euros had been given as subsidies to farmers growing tobacco. There are few crops that are easier to grow than tobacco, particularly on rough and relatively infertile ground. And selling tobacco to developing countries proved hugely profitable.

The end result of this schism was that EUDCE banned smoking but turned a blind eye when its own employees insisted on statutory smoking breaks.

***

Within ten minutes Tom, Dorothy, Dalby and Gladwys had found the perfect site for their meeting; one of many large committee meeting rooms. The room they chose was well equipped with expensive and comfortable furniture. There was no sign here of the poverty and pain that was so widely seen in the world outside. The room's temperature was controlled by a sophisticated air- conditioning system

'Crumbs!' said Tom, looking around. 'People could live in here at night. Out of the cold or the heat.'

'As long as they remembered to get out in time every morning,' said Dalby.

'It'll make a damned good meeting place.'

'Are you sure there are no bugs?' asked Dalby, looking underneath one of the desks and searching for microphones or wiring.

Tom shook his head. 'They would never dare risk it,' he said. 'Not even Europol dare put microphones in here.'

No one working for EUDCE would risk the chance that reports on meetings held in a EUDCE building might somehow be leaked and made available to the suspects. EUDCE commissioners had long memories. They knew about Nixon and Watergate and the role the White House tapes had played in the President's subsequent embarrassment and impeachment. One viewpoint was that he should never have kept the tape recordings. A commoner viewpoint was that he was mad to have authorised them in the first place. Nixon's weakness was his yearning for a place in history; his memoirs; self-justification. But EUDCE was, and always had been, a haven for corruption and theft and the people who worked for it cared only for the now. The truly corrupt and the truly dishonest tend not to think too much about how they will be remembered; they prefer to leave stones where they are lying.

Chapter 29

The meeting began with talk. People airing their complaints in a way they never usually dared to do. They were in a forbidden building. Everyone there was breaking the law. It gave them a bond.

There were many heartfelt complaints.

'I was nearly deported for riding a bicycle without a bell,' complained a slender woman in her twenties. 'I've had three bells stolen in the last six months. And where can you get bells from these days?'

'Steal one,' suggested someone.

'What happened?' asked someone else.

'I bribed him to let me go,' said the girl. She blushed.

'How much did he want?'

'I didn't have any money,' said the girl.

'So how did you bribe him?' asked a tall man with long hair and a port wine stain on his right cheek.

Everyone looked at him.

'Oh,' he said, suddenly embarrassed. 'Oh. I see.'

***

'We had the planners round,' said a woman in her fifties. 'They said our windows were too small. I'd never heard that one before.'

'They brought that law in a couple of months ago,' said a girl with a ponytail. 'They say that windows have to be bigger so that they let in more sunshine and light. They claim it will keep energy usage down and save the planet.'

'It costs a fortune to have windows replaced,' said the tall man.

'Whatever it costs, we can't afford it,' said the woman in her fifties. 'The joke is that we haven't had mains gas or electricity for two years. We don't use any energy. They know that.'

'What did they do?'

'They've given us official notification that if we don't have our windows made larger then we'll be subject to whatever punishment they consider fits the crime.'

'Deportation?'

'I expect so.'

'What are you going to do?'

'We left two nights ago. We're living at my sister's place. It's overcrowded but she was worried that she'd be told to take in some Turks so she's happy. With us living there the sprouts won't put any more people in the flat.'

***

An elderly woman and her husband ('too old to be part of a revolutionary movement but too old to put up with the world as it is,' said the wife) reported that two Amenity Inspectors had come round with cameras to photograph the inside of their home. Councils had been entitled to do this for some years, ostensibly to enable them to decide what local taxes to charge. EUDCE now did it in their place.

'They laughed at every one of our possessions,' said the woman. 'They didn't speak English so I don't know what they were saying. But they just picked our things up and sneered at them. Some things, the things they liked, they put in their pockets. They found a silver photograph frame that belonged to my parents and took out the photograph. They ripped up the photograph and stole the frame.'

'They broke a vase in the bedroom,' said the man. 'I understand what they said then. They said it was ugly.'

The long arm of authority, instead of protecting the public, had become the enemy.

***

'We need to hire some hit men,' said Dalby.

'Like those mercenaries in *The Magnificent Seven*,' said Gladwys.

'That's right,' said Dalby.

'We have to do it ourselves,' said Tom. 'There are too many of them. If we're going to start a revolution then we all need to be involved.'

'I've never killed anyone,' said an old lady. 'Not even a fly.'

'It's true,' said her husband. 'She keeps a kid's fishing net in the house. She catches the flies in that and then releases them.'

'Catches what?' asked Dalby, who hadn't been listening properly.

'Flies,' said the husband.

'None of us are used to killing people,' said Tom. 'But these are exceptional times. We're fighting a war.'

'The people at the bank won't let us have our money,' complained Mrs Tuck. 'They say that since we have a joint account we both have to have passports before they'll let us draw any money out.'

'But what do we need passports for?' asked Mr Tuck, indignantly. 'We can't afford to go anywhere.'

'And we can't afford to buy passports until they let us have our money,' Mrs Tuck pointed out.

'We've had accounts there for forty years,' said Mr Tuck. 'We've been at that bank longer than any of the staff.'

'The man we saw said the bank isn't allowed to give out money without passports,' said Mrs Tuck. 'He said it's to stop terrorism and money laundering.'

'We went to the passport office,' said Mr Tuck. 'They told us that passports would cost us 500 euros each. And we would have to pay in advance.'

'So we can't get our money out,' sighed Mrs Tuck.

***

And there were some surprising admissions.

'I killed a taxman,' said Mrs John.

Everyone stopped and looked at her. Mrs John, whose husband had been a veritable giant of a man, was little more than five foot tall. She could not have weighed more than seven stones.

'He came to the house and demanded to see my husband's accounts,' said Mrs John. 'They'd been chasing him for two years. It killed him, you know. The letters. They threatened all sorts of terrible things.'

She opened her handbag, took out a small, light-blue, linen handkerchief and wiped her eyes. 'He paid them everything he owed. Probably more than he owed. He was a very honest man. He hardly earned enough to keep us alive but he always paid his taxes. But still they wouldn't listen. They always wanted more documents. More receipts. More paper.'

'How did you kill the taxman?' asked Dalby quietly.

'He came round just a week after my Geoffrey's funeral,' said Mrs John. 'They wouldn't leave him alone even then. They wanted to see a receipt for something he'd bought six years ago. They said they were going to arrest him and deport him.'

'Did you tell them he was...'

'I told him Geoffrey had passed on and he said they'd arrest me and that would be Geoffrey's legacy to me,' said Mrs John. 'That made me very cross. My Geoffrey would have been angry that they said that. So I took the man up to the attic where Geoffrey kept all the old receipts and then I came downstairs and I locked the hatch into the attic and I left him there.'

'Didn't he make a noise? Shout and bang?'

'Oh yes. He made a lot of noise. He shouted and threatened and banged on the floor. But we live several hundred yards away from anyone else. And Geoffrey made the hatch himself. It's very strong. And he boarded up the roof on the inside to keep out the wind.'

'How long ago did this happen?'

'It was a week after Geoffrey died. Just seven months ago now.'

'Have you been back up into the attic?' Mrs John shook her head. 'No.'

'And no one else came to see you?'

'Two men from the tax people came. They wanted to know if I'd seen the man they'd sent before. They showed me his picture. I told them it looked like my cousin who used to live in Great Yarmouth but who died on the trawlers back in the days when there were such things. I told them my husband had died and that I didn't know what they were talking about and they went away.'

For a while no one spoke.

***

'So, what the hell are we going to do about it?' demanded Will Stutely. 'Are we just going to sit around all night and tell each other horror stories? Or are we going to decide to do something? Mrs John has showed us the way.'

Silence.

'You'd better say something,' whispered Dorothy to Tom.

'What?' asked Tom.

'Just talk,' said Dorothy. 'Something will come to you.'

Chapter 30

Tom stood up and walked to the front of the room.

'Things are the way they are because too many of us said and did nothing for too long,' he said. He felt nervous but too angry to care. He was talking to about thirty people. All hand-picked. All angry. All ready for the revolution. He looked around and suddenly realised that there were few people under fifty in the room. Young people thought that they were revolting if they took drugs, dyed their hair green and sat around all day drinking home-made potato wine. Years of living in a world run by EUDCE had taken the heart and soul out of them. They did not understand that the bureaucrats, paid to protect the innocent, had become the enemy; that they were now the ones against whom the citizens needed protection; that authority had become the mask of violence.

'The sprouts who work for EUDCE are not our friends and not on our side. They have been bought by large salaries (far greater than anything they could have ever earned in the real world) and index-linked pensions and a good deal of power. And oh, how they love the power. Think back to how it started. The security guards at airports, there to protect us from terrorists. But did they ever catch anyone? Did they ever prevent any tragedy? No and no again. They were dumb, unskilled idiots. No skills. They just loved ordering people around. Think of the dustmen refusing to take your rubbish because you'd put a yoghurt carton in with the egg boxes. They loved the power. Our present tormentors are the same people. But they're paid more and treated better and they have become the 'them' we always feared would one day take over our lives.'

'We should be able to put EUDCE and its bureaucrats on trial for the crimes they have committed in our name. But we can't.'

'We can't get rid of them by voting them out because they offer us no alternative. We can't demonstrate in the streets because they've banned that. We can't get rid of them with an ordinary, old-fashioned revolution because they own all the weapons worth having. We can't kill the leaders as the people usually do in revolutions because they are too well guarded. Our only option is to start at the bottom and work our way up.'

'We trusted the people who had the power because it never occurred to us that they would betray us and lie to us and use us. We trusted them too much because we did not understand how much people will cheat in order to obtain money and power. We were more innocent, more naive, than we thought we were. We judged them by the same standards we were accustomed to using when judging our friends, our relations and the people we meet at work and in the shops. In our normal daily lives we try to be a little cautious, and we assume that we can judge when people are lying to us. We have all met people who cheat a little or lie a little. But we have little experience of people who cheat all the time and whose every word, every promise, every reassurance is a blatant lie. We have little experience of such uncompromising deceit. And so we trusted when we should not have trusted. We believed when we should not have believed.'

'Like the ordinary Germans in the 1930's, we trusted too much. That was our original crime, if you want to call it that. We said nothing, allowing our country to be stolen from us. Now, we know that complaining won't do us any good. We either have to live with what has happened or we have to do something about it ourselves. In my view, living with it has become impossible, unbearable and close to pointless. And so we have to do something.'

'It's too late to change things with talk or persuasion. We live in a world where we no longer have the rights we used to have; the rights we believed we would always have. Everything we valued; our freedom, our history, our culture, has been stolen from us by people who looked us straight in the eye and made promises they had no intention of keeping; people who, with honest faces, made assurances they knew were untrue. They've taken our past, our present and our future.'

'I am in mourning for my country because the life and soul have been taken from it. When they take your country from you they take your identity. We have been deprived of our birthright, our pride, our passion and our sense of belonging. And what have we been given in exchange? Would any one of us fight for EUDCE?'

'They have given us a world in which social engineering programmes such as means-testing, political correctness and multiculturalism are used as weapons to oppress us. They have given us a world in which health and safety bureaucrats create rules not to make the world a safer place but to enhance their own power and status and end up making the world more dangerous than it was before. For years we have all pushed aside our fears and our sense of injustice, not because we felt that our fears were unfounded or because our sense of injustice was misplaced, but because deep down we felt that we could do nothing to change things: we knew that justice and the law had been separated. And so we suppressed our feeling that things were wrong and just put up with our lives.'

'We have been betrayed by people who pretended to care about us, men and women who claimed to be driven by a desire to serve, but who cared only about themselves. We have been cheated by people whose ambitions were purely personal, materialistic and oh so very, very selfish. We have been betrayed by people who sold us out in return for chauffeur-driven cars, unlimited expense accounts and huge pensions.'

'And now it is too late to change things by what we say or how we vote. We have sleepwalked into defeat; we have wandered, perhaps innocently, perhaps a little stupidly, into a fascist world where we no longer have any say in our destiny or our children's destiny. Our mistake was to believe what we were told. The consequences are around us every day and unless we now accept the existence of the problem, and the fact that our destiny is in our hands, we can never defeat those who oppress us.'

'You could argue, not unreasonably, that our quarrel should be with those who have done these things to us; those whom we trusted and who then lied to us, cheated us and betrayed us. You could sensibly claim that our quarrel is with the politicians who signed the treaties which gave away our rights, our freedoms, our democracy, our culture and our independence.'

'But such an argument doesn't get us very far. Most of those who signed those treaties are dead or dying or rich and in hiding – well protected and beyond our reach. They will have to pay the price for their disloyalty and their greed in some other jurisdiction. But, the truth is that revenge against them will change nothing. We could dig up the ones who died, try them for treason and then hang them. We could drag the ones who are still alive out of their beds and into the courts but doing so would change nothing.'

'Our war now must be against the institution they created. But what is an institution? What is there to fight? The institution is represented by buildings. We could blow them up, but what difference would that make? They would shoot us all and then put up more buildings. Nothing would change. The institution is run by the commissioners and the senior bureaucrats. They serve the institution. They are well guarded. What happens if we manage to break through the security and kill the leaders? Nothing. The institution now has a life of its own. The institution will merely recruit more commissioners and more bureaucrats. It will have no difficulty in finding people prepared to accept the lifestyle enjoyed by the commissioners and the bureaucrats. Our lives will not be improved one jot by removing these people. We will still be oppressed. We will still live in fear. We will still live in poverty. We will be manacled by rules and regulations which govern our every movement and we will live in a joyless, hopeless world; denied a history and denied a future by colourless, faceless, unelected bureaucrats. The next generation of commissioners and bureaucrats will simply introduce more rules and more regulations and more policemen in order to ensure that we do not rise up again. We will be worse off than before.'

'So, what can we do?'

'There is only one answer. There is only one way forward. We have to eliminate the people who act for and on behalf of the institution; we have to destroy the people who represent the institution, the people without whom the institution cannot function.'

'The sprouts, the people who control our movements and who terrorise us on a daily basis, are the arms and legs of the institution. If we remove them then the institution will try to find replacements. But it cannot do this indefinitely. When it becomes clear that working as a sprout is a dangerous occupation there will be fewer applicants for the work. The institution may be able to protect the commissioners and the senior bureaucrats with guards and guns and razor wire and high walls. But it cannot protect the sprouts who represent it in our communities. The institution cannot protect the men and women who come into our homes, abuse us, take what little we have, sneer at us, invade our privacy and steal what little dignity we have left. Our only possible targets are those who work with and for the fascist Eurostate as its oh-so-willing servants of terror – they are, to us, the true terrorists of our age. Without them the State would have no teeth.'

'I look around the world in which we now live and I want to scream in rage and frustration. I see poverty and unhappiness and hopelessness. I see rules and regulations created without thought, compassion or reason. I see corruption, prejudice and cruelty. I see a two-tone world in which the haves are the people who work for the State and the rest of us are the have-nots. I see good, honest soldiers dying in wars which are being fought so that politicians and bureaucrats and company directors can steal commodities from poor nations and make themselves rich. I see people being killed by the police officers who are paid to protect them. I see governments imprisoning innocent people and torturing them in our name. I see protests suppressed and protestors oppressed. I see all this, every day. I see it getting worse, every day.'

'The time has come for a revolution. And we must not fail. We will not get a second chance. We must change things and not just rearrange them. We are at war with an invader just as much as at any time in our history. Those who work with EUDCE are collaborators and history will show them to be the traitors they are; as treacherous as any who worked with the Nazis in the Second World War. The fascist foot soldiers always enjoy the perks of their positions but they must now endure the vicissitudes and, if necessary, pay the penalty. If we kill enough of them then fewer will come forward to replace them and the power structure of EUDCE, built on fear and oppression, will slowly but surely crumble.'

'During the Second World War our grandfathers and our fathers didn't just try to kill Hitler, Goering and the other leaders. They tried their hardest to kill every German they could get their hands on. In a war there are no civilians. Possibly the greatest single military achievement of the Second World War, the one that inspired the loudest and longest lasting patriotic fervour, was the Dam Busters raid. Did anyone then stop to worry about the fact that the raid resulted in the flooding of vast acreages of German countryside and the inevitable death by drowning of countless German citizens? Did the pilots drown only German servicemen? Of course they didn't.'

'We, in contrast, are targeting and killing only those who are our active enemies. We won't kill good people; only bureaucrats and state thugs. Ours has become an everyday story of gentle folk who have to kill. These aren't just petty, low-level functionaries sent round to check that the labels in our underclothes don't contain imperial measurements; these are the soldiers of an oppressive, invading army which has taken over our lives, our country and our world.'

'If you believe that I have spoken the truth then you must stay and be with us. If you believe that what I have said is either untrue or unrealistic then you must leave. If you leave then I cannot and will not try to stop you reporting what I have said to the sprouts. But if you leave then you must accept the world as it is now; a world that is deteriorating still; a world which offers us no hope and no future.'

'We are all here because we're fed up of whingeing but doing nothing. It's time to stop moaning and to start taking action.'

'And we must ask ourselves two questions. First, if not us, then who? And second, if not now, then when?'

Tom sat down.

For a long, long moment there was silence.

No one spoke. No one clapped. No one cheered. Just silence.

He felt a hand holding his. He looked across at Dorothy and smiled. She squeezed his fingers.

Silence.

Suddenly, Tom's aunt stood up and started to clap. She did so without warning and she clapped ferociously, with massive enthusiasm. Immediately, a short man on the second row stood up too. He was in his forties. He wore a sports jacket frayed at the cuffs and worn at the collar. The buttons which had once doubtless decorated the cuffs were missing. Two of the three buttons used to fasten the jacket were gone. He stood there and Dorothy could see that tears were rolling down his cheeks. He raised his hands high in the air and he clapped hard, loud and long.

And within an instant everyone in the room was standing and clapping and cheering. Many were crying. Some were smiling at one another. There were thirty people in the room. No more. But they made as much noise as a crowd ten, one hundred times, bigger.

Tom watched the back door to see if anyone left. If one person left the room they would all have to leave quickly. The moment and the mood would be gone. As would hope.

But no one left.

'Bravo,' murmured Dalby, who was standing next to Tom. He too was clapping. 'Did you memorise all that? I didn't see you use any notes?'

'I didn't prepare anything,' said Tom, who was in a daze. 'I didn't have any notes.' Tom was now the only person sitting. He wasn't sure whether he should stand. But when he tried to get up his legs would not work.

Dalby bent down. 'So, where did all that come from?' he asked. 'You said things which really struck a chord.'

'Just from the heart,' said Tom. 'From the heart,' he repeated. He had spoken with a passion even he had not known he felt and now he was utterly drained.

He had sold them a revolution.

A small one, perhaps, but a revolution nevertheless.

Chapter 31

There were questions, many questions.

'Why can't we fight them in the courts?' asked Jan Stewer, a small man in an old but well-looked after suit.

'We can't sue them because they made the laws. They made all the rules. The Lisbon Treaty, and everything that came after it, took away all our basic rights. And we can't sue them or take them to court because years ago, before it became EUDCE, the European Union gave itself, its officers and all its employees complete immunity from the law. The people who work for EUDCE have total authority without any responsibility. And so, since we are denied the opportunity to use the law we must go outside the law to find our answer.'

'Let's get down to practicalities,' said a middle-aged woman called Edith Gurney who wore a floral print dress and a hat with flowers on the side. She looked like the sort of woman who would have been more at home making jam. 'What, precisely, are you asking us to do?' She asked this as though she were asking for a recipe for sponge cake.

'There are only two aspects to the work we have to do. First, we have to kill the sprouts. And then we have to do something with the bodies. Of the two, getting rid of the bodies is the bigger problem. The killing itself you should aim to keep as simple as possible. The best way to kill a sprout is to hit them on the head with something solid and rather heavy – the traditional blunt instrument so beloved of detective story writers. This method has the advantage that if something happens between the killing and the disposal, the death can be more easily 'sold' as an accident than if you, say, resort to poisoning or electrocution. It would be nigh on impossible to persuade the authorities that a sprout had died after taking an accidental overdose of weed killer. It will be easier to persuade them that a sprout fell down some stairs or tripped over an uneven bit of pavement and hit his head on a kerbstone. It will be easier because that's what they will prefer to believe.'

'Why can't we get guns?' asked Peter Day. 'We could steal them.'

'There is no point in our dreaming of a revolution with guns,' said Tom. 'What can we get? Target pistols? A few double barrel shotguns? An airgun or two? Maybe even a machine gun? EUDCE has rocket launchers, bombers, gunship helicopters, destroyers, aircraft carriers, tanks, cruise missiles, nuclear submarines, chemical and biological weapons and an army, a navy and an air force. The bureaucrats within EUDCE have unlimited resources to throw at us if we declare war the way they fight wars. We cannot fight EUDCE with guns because we'll lose. They will always have the biggest and most powerful weapons.' Tom paused. 'Now can anyone suggest suitable blunt instruments that might be lying around the average home?'

'I think I heard someone mention saucepans. Is that because they have a convenient handle?' asked a plump woman called Mrs Pearse. She wore a dress that was several sizes too small for her. Her husband Tom had been a bank manager in what most people now called 'the olden days'. He, like Tom Cobleigh, now worked as a part-time allotment guard and was just as glad of the work.

'A saucepan or frying pan is good as long as it's heavy,' replied Tom Cobleigh. 'Don't use a light aluminium one. It will probably just bounce off the sprout's skull without doing him much harm. The last thing you want is a surprised and annoyed sprout who is still on his feet. And don't pick a weapon with a flimsy handle.'

'What about a shoe or heavy boot?' asked Mrs Pearse.

'No, I don't think so. A heavy boot might give someone a headache but that's not really what we're aiming for here.'

'A chair? A wooden chair?' suggested Bill Brewer, a former sales representative for a motor car company. His job had gone when the car industry had died. 'The sort of thing you might find in a kitchen or a dining room.' He had hair that looked like a toupee but wasn't. If he'd been a grocery item he would have long before passed his sell-by date.

'A chair can be good but only if you have enough space to swing it properly. You'd probably be surprised to find out how difficult it is to swing a chair in an ordinary kitchen. There just isn't enough room.' Tom picked up a chair and showed what he meant by trying to raise it above his head. The chair clattered into a light shade. He lowered it amidst some uncertain laughter. 'You'll probably also find that chairs may be rather heavy and difficult to aim properly,' he added.

'A cricket bat? Baseball bat?' This suggestion came from Harry Hawk. Once a professional violinist with a large orchestra, Mr Hawk now collected and sold firewood to earn a living.

'Splendid!' agreed Tom – who would only later realise how surreal it was that he had somehow become regarded as an expert on killing instruments. 'But you might find a cricket bat a little too large for indoor use. And don't forget that cricket is an outlawed game. So if you have a cricket bat in the house make sure that you keep it hidden until you want to use it!'

'How about a golf club?' asked, an elderly man in a Garrick club tie. Since no one played golf any more (partly because there were no golf courses and no way of getting to them even if there had been) there were plenty of golf clubs available. Many suspects used them as walking sticks and 'defenders'; the best way to fight off stray dogs.

'Maybe too long for indoor use,' suggested Tom.

'How hard should we hit?'

'As hard as you can.'

'Pity we can't kill them with paper. A ton of paper suddenly landing on top of them.'

Everyone looked.

'That's what they do to us.'

Everyone nodded understanding. There were some smiles.

'Strangle them with red tape,' suggested Peter Day.

There were chuckles of approval.

'Getting back to the use of blunt objects,' said Daniel Whiddon. 'Do you recommend that we hold the weapon in any particular way? As a former Health and Safety Executive Officer I am concerned that we might sustain wrist or lower arm injuries if we use ergonomically unsound methods when wielding our weapons.'

'Just hold it tight and bring it down hard,' said Tom, trying hard not to smile. Daniel Whiddon was one of the many former civil servants who hadn't been employed as a sprout. Most of the plum jobs had been given to Europeans from the East of the new European Superstate.

'Do you favour a one-handed grip or a two-handed grip?'

'I hadn't really thought about a two-handed grip,' admitted Tom. 'You're thinking of perhaps holding, say, a saucepan in the way that some people used to hold a tennis racket?'

'That sort of thing, yes.' As far as Tom knew no one had played tennis for years. A few higher echelon sprouts probably still played on private courts. But there were no courts for suspects to use. Sports were considered too confrontational for suspects to take part in.

'I'm not sure about that,' admitted Tom. 'I think it's probably up to the individual to find a grip that he feels comfortable with. Maybe it would be worth doing a little practising beforehand.'

'Or she,' said a woman in the front row whom Tom did not recognise.

'I beg your pardon?'

'You said 'find a grip that he feels comfortable with'. You should have said 'find a grip that he or she feels comfortable with'.'

'Of course. I'm sorry. A grip that he or she feels comfortable with. But it all depends to a certain extent on the weapon you've picked up. And it's not always possible to know in advance precisely what you'll be using.'

'What part of the body do you recommend as a target?'

'Always the head. That's your target.'

'Front, back or sides?'

'Sounds like a haircut!' There was some sniggering from the left of the room.

'Doesn't matter,' said Tom. 'Whatever is easiest to reach. Don't waste time trying to manoeuvre yourself into a position to hit him, or indeed her, on the back of the head.'

'Should we kill female sprouts too?'

'Of course. It would be against sex discrimination legislation for us not to kill female sprouts,' said the woman in the front row before Tom could speak.

'Just go ahead and hit,' said Tom. 'And make sure that you hit hard. The first hit probably won't kill him but it should stun him. Then you can finish him off at your leisure. Or her,' he added, with a glance at the woman in the front row. 'Get a good swing and really bash him hard. You're not patting him as you'd pat a dog. You need to get some real movement into your arm. And remember that female skulls can be just as thick as male skulls. So don't hold back just because you're killing a female sprout. And remember, you aren't aiming to win marks for style. The aim is simply to kill the sprout as quickly as possible and to then dispose of the body.'

'What about other methods of killing?' asked Harry Hawk. 'Electrocution, for example.'

'I think that might prove rather too complicated.'

'Poison? Give the sprout some home-made cake that contains arsenic.'

'It would take too long,' said Dalby, who hadn't spoken for a while. 'And if anyone did find the body and examine it they'd know that he was murdered.'

'Inject him with a lethal dose of heroin.'

'Where are we going to get heroin from?' said Dalby. 'And we'd have to hold him down while we injected him. If we've already got him under control why bother injecting him?'

'We could run him over with a car,' suggested Jan Stewer.

'We'd have to steal a car first. And then persuade the sprout to stand still while we ran him over. Sprouts are not the world's most intelligent people but I can't see any of them doing that.'

'We could arrange for the sprout to be bitten by a rabid dog,' suggested Mrs Brewer.

'Do you have a rabid dog?' asked Peter Day.

'Not at the moment, no. But there must be some around.'

'I could seduce him and then tell his wife,' said Harry Hawk's mother, who had been in her eighties for as long as Tom Cobleigh could remember.

'How would that help?'

'She'd kill him!'

'How do you know that?'

'Well, I would if he were my husband.'

'She might not care. She might even be glad he's having an affair. She might be having an affair herself. Besides, it will take too much time for you to seduce him and tell his wife and for her to beat him to death with a poker or whatever.'

'I hadn't thought of that.'

'We have to keep this simple. We're amateurs but they're all arrogant bastards and none of them expects anyone to kill them. We don't need any equipment or anything complicated. Just hit them hard on the head or push them down the stairs. One or the other.'

'Or both,' said Peter Gurney.

'Or both, if required,' agreed Tom with a quiet smile.

Chapter 32

At the end of the meeting they left the building one at a time, leaving at thirty second intervals. Tom, who was the last to leave, didn't see the sprouts until the car screeched to a halt and the two of them leapt out and suddenly appeared in front of him. His first thought was relief that he had sent Dorothy home ahead of him.

Despite the fuel shortages some of the police sprouts still drove around in cars. They used a fleet of identical (and therefore easily identified) dark blue Ford Smegmas. In a vain attempt to confuse the public, and to disguise the appearance of the cars, some had dark green upholstery while some had dark blue. It wasn't much of a disguise.

Instead of the usual sprout suits the two who jumped out of the car wore bullet and knife proof jackets and balaclavas made of the same material. They were Community Protection Officers, the most feared of all sprouts. Over their balaclavas they wore goggles. They looked as fierce and as frightening as they were. They were known to be aggressive and prone to violence. Both the sprouts carried long nightsticks. Made of steel these could easily break any bone in the human body with a single blow. They were also armed with Uzi machine guns and taser guns.

'Where are you going?' demanded the fatter of the two Protection Officers. Other than by the slight difference in their bulk it was impossible to distinguish between the two. Neither wore numbers or any form of identification. The sprout's balaclava had slipped a little and was half across his mouth. His words were slightly muffled but just comprehensible.

'Home, sir,' replied Tom. It annoyed him to have to add the 'sir' to his reply. But if it saved him a one way trip to Africa it was a price worth paying. He remembered that in the olden times a policeman would address members of the public as 'sir' or 'madam'.

'Where's home?' demanded the Protection Officer.

'Just half a mile down the road, sir,' said Tom, pointing in the direction he was heading.

It wasn't a mistake. He said it deliberately.

Foolishly he hadn't prepared an answer to the question he knew they would ask next: 'Where have you been?' He could hardly tell them where he'd really been. And there was a good chance that a lie would be too easy to spot. Without an instantly believable answer to that question they would arrest him. He would be on the boat to Africa before dawn. And so he deliberately distracted them, enraged them, by using an imperial measurement. Half a mile. It was the red rag. But it stopped the questioning.

The sprouts' response was entirely as he had expected but it came surprisingly quickly. Nevertheless, the fact that he was expecting it meant that Tom was able to take the blow on his forearm, rather than his skull. The crack of the radial bone as it broke was loud; actually audible. His scream of pain was louder. The pain was genuine but Tom didn't try to hide his distress. His only chance, he knew, was that the sprouts might be satisfied with breaking just one bone. If he showed no sign of pain they would continue beating him until he did. Pity would not save him. Contempt might. He could live with their contempt.

'How far is it? How far is it?' demanded the second Protection Officer. The one who had not yet spoken.

'Less than a kilometre, sir,' sobbed Tom. He clutched his arm and rocked backwards and forwards slightly. He did not sink to his knees. If you did that the sprouts would sometimes find the opportunity to beat you around the head quite irresistible. He had to protect his head and so he stayed standing. But he sobbed and whined and moaned and was as pitiful as he could be. Unworthy of their further attention.

'That's better,' said the Protection Officer who had struck the blow.

'Snivelling bastard,' said the other.

And then they were gone. Walking away, laughing together, back to their car.

Tom didn't wait. Holding his broken arm he hurried home as fast as he could go.

***

The break wasn't as bad as it might have been.

'Thank heavens it was a simple fracture,' said Dorothy. A neighbour, a doctor, set the fracture, and put on a plaster of Paris cast.

'I'm not going to be able to kill anyone for weeks,' complained Tom.

'It's your left arm,' Dorothy pointed out.
'I'll never be able to move the bodies,' said Tom.
'Then give some tutorials,' suggested Dorothy.
Frowning in puzzlement, Tom looked at her. 'What on earth on?'
'Murder,' replied Dorothy simply.

Chapter 33

Tom's killing tutorials quickly became enormously popular. If he had been a university lecturer he would have been the faculty star.

The first tutorial was held in their tiny living room. But by the second tutorial it was clear that this simply wouldn't work.

'You could try the EUDCE offices again,' suggested Dorothy.

'I'm never going back in there!' insisted Tom. 'We can only use them at night. And the last time I came back from there I was lucky to escape with a broken arm.'

So they held the tutorials in the park where, if anyone stopped and wanted to know what they were doing, Tom pretended he was teaching t'ai chi classes.

'If you break an arm or a leg he can still come at you and if he is angry and determined, which he will be, he may still kill you. You have one huge advantage: surprise. And you must use that to full effect so that you take him out of the game as quickly as possible. The only way to do this is to hit him hard on the head, thereby rendering him incapable of doing you harm, however strong and determined he may be. The sprout who is unconscious, or at the very least dizzy and confused is far less of a threat than, say, the sprout with a broken arm. You have to raise your weapon to at least his head height. What's the easy way to do that?'

'Stand on a chair?' suggested someone.

Tom sighed and closed his eyes for a moment. 'No,' he said, patiently. 'Get him to sit down. Offer him a cup of tea or whatever you have to offer. Flatter him. Flirt with him. Promise him or her some or more of whatever it is that you think he or she might like.'

Tom wondered sometimes how many people outside the armed forces had given tutorials in murder.

Chapter 34

Tom, Dorothy, Dalby, Gladwys and the rest knew that killing sprouts was only half the problem.

The other half of the problem was getting rid of the bodies.

Working on the basis that the best place to hide a needle is in a sewing basket, and the best place to hide money is in a bank, they resurrected Tom's original idea and began by hiding bodies in the few local cemeteries that were still functioning as cemeteries and which had not been turned into allotments.

This worked well for a while. Once they had found out when graves were being dug it wasn't too difficult to sneak in at night, dig a little deeper, drop in a body and cover it with a thin layer of soil. On half a dozen occasions they managed to open up family vaults and drop in a couple of visitors.

'Nice to have a bit of fresh blood in there,' said Dalby. 'Otherwise the inbreeding will result in a lower grade of ghoul.'

But they found that there was a limit to the number of times they could do this without arousing suspicions.

They finally gave up using graveyards when they heard that two separate firms of undertakers had made representations to the authorities about strange things happening to dug graves. 'Someone's part filling them up!' a gravedigger had complained, after two of Tom's students didn't dig deep enough, and failed to leave enough room for the coffin for which the grave had originally been created. 'We dug it plenty deep enough.'

They then tried using a graveyard which had been turned into allotments.

'The soil there is much easier to dig,' explained Tom. 'It's been well-manured and dug over so it's easy to dig down and create a grave. The soil is softer and easier to work. It really is the best place to dig.'

All would have been well if some of the allotment holders hadn't been so keen. When an enthusiastic gardener unearthed a body while preparing to plant his potatoes the would-be revolutionaries abandoned that idea too.

An attempt to get rid of bodies by grinding them up, spreading them over the ground and digging them in proved time-consuming, exhausting, messy and woefully ineffective. There were rumours of fingers and bits of bone being found.

A man who ran a private crematorium for pets (called *Pets to Powder*) helped for a while but most of his customers were sprouts (suspects couldn't possibly afford to pay to have their pets cremated) and they began to ask questions about the vast quantities of ash being produced. After a woman sprout who had taken in a pet poodle complained that her pet weighed twice as much dead as he had done alive the crematorium owner told Tom that although he was with them in spirit they couldn't use his furnaces any longer.

Attempts to get a licence for a landfill site were almost abandoned when the application forms turned up. They weighed as much as a large dog and were far more terrifying. The application finally faltered at the point where they had to admit that they were not intending to bury American radioactive rubbish in their landfill site. Thanks to a treaty between the USA and EUDCE this was, apparently, a non-negotiable requirement.

They got rid of a couple of dozen bodies by chopping them up and putting the remains into the garbage cans behind restaurants favoured by higher echelon sprouts. This seemed a good idea but two things went wrong. A chef at one of the restaurants had a nice sideline selling the contents of the bins to a dealer who used the scraps as raw ingredients in his pie making business. The dealer wasn't a bright man but after three of his customers found wedding rings in their pies even his suspicions were aroused. 'There are human body parts in your bins!' he complained to the chef. Almost simultaneously, a stray dog pulled an arm out of a bin and was spotted dragging it along the pavement outside the front of the restaurant. A sprout passing by noticed the expensive, diamond-studded, solid gold Rolex watch still ticking on the disconnected wrist. After that a guard was put on garbage cans and this particular method of disposal had to end.

And then, for a while, they got rid of bodies by taking them along to the official recycling centre.

On the night they started this method of disposal, Tom and Dalby were heading for a lake where they had dumped bodies once or twice. It was late, it was dark and it was raining when they found themselves passing an authorised EUDCE tip. They had four bodies in the trailers behind their two bicycles. Both Tom and Dalby were exhausted. Riding a bicycle which is towing a dead body is like riding a tandem with one of the riders doing no pedalling. Riding a bicycle which is towing two dead bodies is twice as hard.

They both stopped for a rest.

'How much further is the lake?'

'Another five miles at least.'

They said nothing for a while, both of them staring at the huge sign which announced that they were standing outside EUDCE's official recycling tip no 148273.

'Are you thinking...'

'I am.'

'Which bin do we put them in?' asked Tom, looking around. The tip was divided into dozens of sections. There were bins for electrical appliances, plain glass bottles, brown bottles, green bottles and so on.

'This one,' said Dalby, who was peering at the list of acceptable contents at the side of a huge metal container. There was a ramp leading up the side of the container so that suspects could throw in their rubbish.

'What's it for?'

'It's for unwanted vegetable remnants,' said Dalby. 'Potatoes, cauliflowers, carrots, cabbages, onions and sprouts!'

'Perfect!' agreed Tom.

They dragged the sprouts up the ramp and tossed them into the rotting compost below, hoping that the next suspects to use the bin would simply tip their unwanted vegetables on top of what was there without looking down, and that if they did look down they would not call one of the sprouts to tell him what they'd seen.

On a subsequent visit they even popped small sprouts into bottle banks (a process which would, in the olden days, have aroused considerable interest among the tabloid press but which didn't even merit a mention on the Telescreen). This worked well for a couple of weeks. But bodies were spotted and extra sprouts were stationed at all refuse dumps, even when they were officially closed.

'We're attracting too much attention,' said Tom one day. 'The aim is to kill and get rid of the bodies as quietly as we can. If we arouse too much interest then we'll be stopped. We need to hide the bodies so that they aren't found.'

'That's easier to say than do,' pointed out Gladwys.

Chapter 35

They devised a new way to confuse Europol.

Every time a sprout was dispatched, the killers removed any identification and passed it to Dorothy. And, every weekend, when the hospital was at its quietest, Dorothy would walk in, taking with her the week's accumulation of identity cards. She would walk straight through the casualty department and log onto the computer in the ward sister's office. Through the hospital computer she would access the national sprout register and delete the details of the sprouts they had killed. Click, click, click, they were gone for ever from the database. They did not exist. And they never had. No one could have been murdered because no one existed in the first place. The computer enabled Tom, Dorothy and the others to commit perfect crimes.

'You can't argue with the computer,' workmates of the missing sprouts would be told. 'We have no one of that name on record.'

'But I worked with him for six years!'

'You must be mistaken. You can't argue with the computer.'

Chapter 36

The big problem remained: how to get rid of the bodies.
    And then a solution arrived from a thoroughly unexpected quarter.

Chapter 37

They wanted to ignore whoever it was who was knocking on the door. But the unknown visitor was determined. He, she or they knocked on the door for twenty five minutes.

'They're not going to go away,' whispered Dorothy eventually.

'Give them five more minutes,' suggested Tom.

They were standing in the hallway and they were whispering so that whoever was at the door wouldn't know they were there.

For a few minutes everything was quiet.

'I think they've gone away,' whispered Dorothy. And then the banging started at the back door.

'I'll open it,' said Tom with a sigh.

'We thought you were in,' said the first sprout. He was a small, swarthy looking man with a sharp, long nose and black hair combed forward. He looked as though he'd been carrying the troubles of the world on his shoulders for centuries. Tom thought he looked a little like Napoleon Bonaparte.

'When we pushed open the letter box we could see you and hear you whispering,' said the second sprout. He was taller, stouter and younger. He had a poor complexion and looked like a man who enjoyed bad food.

'Are you Dorothy Cobleigh?' asked Napoleon.

Dorothy admitted that she was. It seemed too late to pretend otherwise.

'The sculptress?'

'Sculptor,' said Dorothy. 'I prefer sculptor.'

'We were told sculptress,' said the stout sprout. 'So if you don't mind we'll stick to that. We had a hell of a job finding you.'

'Someone very important wants to see you,' said Napoleon. 'We were asked to collect you and take you to EUDCE Headquarters.' He paused. 'If it's convenient to you,' he added. He smiled. It was a scary sort of smile. 'We were told to say that,' he said.

'Oh dear,' said Dorothy. She wasn't sure whether this was good news or bad news but the odds seemed heavily on bad.

'Do you know what they want?' asked Tom.

'No idea at all,' said Napoleon. 'We're just the collectors.'

'So, is it convenient?' asked the stout sprout.

'Can I change my shoes?' asked Dorothy.

'Of course,' said Napoleon. 'Take all the time you like.' He looked at his watch.

'Can I go with her?' asked Tom.

The stout sprout looked at his companion. 'Don't see why not,' said Napoleon.

Chapter 38

They travelled in style since the Chief Commissioner had sent one of her fleet of official Rolls Royce cars to collect the sculptor. (In addition to her private collection of motor cars, the Chief Commissioner also had a fleet of six Rolls Royce limousines at her disposal.)

Sitting in the back of the car Tom and Dorothy watched a Telescreen programme in which ten contestants had to use their olfactory skills to assess the faeces which had been produced by an unnamed celebrity, and to then decide what five foods the celebrity had eaten in the previous 48 hours. The winner, the contestant who got the most foods right, suggested 'cranberries, garlic and parsnip' but missed prunes and celery. He had been practising for nine months using his wife, workmates and neighbours as research assistants. He won a surgical operation in a sprout hospital.

'Surgical operations are popular prizes these days,' said Tom.

'Pity you can't have the operation you want,' said Dorothy. 'Or store up the prize until you need it.'

At the EUDCE Headquarters building Dorothy and Tom were ushered into the entrance hall where a receptionist sat at a massive oak desk upon which stood nothing but a single telephone. Two busby-wearing soldiers, one at each end of the desk, stood on guard outside smartly painted wooden sentry boxes. Dorothy thought they looked like something W. S. Gilbert might have dreamt up as an adornment for one of his Savoy operettas.

'Dorothy Cobleigh for Sir Czardas Tsastske,' said Napoleon, addressing the receptionist. The other sprout, the stout one, had stayed in the Rolls Royce so that he could drive it back to the garage. The Chief Commissioner liked her cars to be given a full wax and polish after every use.

The receptionist picked up her telephone, dialled 0 and waited. She then asked to be put through to Sir Czardas's receptionist. Two minutes later she put the telephone back on its cradle, and waved an imperious and immaculately manicured hand in the direction of the lifts.

'Third floor,' she said, speaking with an accent Dorothy couldn't place.

'I thought we'd be seeing someone on one of the upper floors,' said Tom, as they headed towards the lifts. He was feeling more confident now. The back of the limousine had been equipped with a bar, and it was the very presence of the bar, as much as the alcohol he had drunk on the journey, which had made Tom feel comfortable. It seemed unlikely to him that a journey in a car fitted with a bar could end completely badly. 'Don't important people usually have their offices on their top floors?'

'The top brass only use the first three floors,' replied Napoleon. He turned and lowered his voice, sharing a secret. 'The lifts don't always work.'

'Ah,' nodded Tom, understanding. It was nice to know that the sprouts had their little problems too.

They got into the lift. There were seats inside. An attendant in a smart blue and gold uniform, including a blue and gold peaked cap with an impressive looking badge on the front, greeted them with a salute.

Out of the corner of a disobedient eye the lift attendant was watching his favourite Telescreen programme, a daily soap opera which told the story of a saintly black, gay Romanian who had a lisp, a limp and an ugly dog.

'Third floor,' said Napoleon.

'Certainly sir,' said the attendant, with obvious reluctance, tearing the corner of the disobedient eye off the screen in order to concentrate. 'Please take your seats and fasten your seat belts.'

Tom and Dorothy looked at the seats and then at the lift attendant.

'Health and safety rules,' the attendant explained. He spoke English with a heavy accent and Tom and Dorothy had difficulty understanding him. 'I can't press the button until you fasten your belts.'

They sat down and fastened their belts.

Standing in front of them, and holding himself firmly to attention, the lift attendant then took a small laminated card and a pair of reading spectacles out of his top pocket. He put on the spectacles and read to them the words printed on the card.

'In case of an emergency malfunction of the suspension mechanisms, air bags will be liberated from the floor and sides of the elevator capsule. Liftees are to stay still and calm and remain in their seats to await rescue. In case of a door opening failure, emergency supplies of vitamins and nuts can be found available underneath your seats. These may contain vitamins and traces of nuts.'

'Life's full of ups and downs, eh,' said Tom. Dorothy glanced at him and dug him in the ribs with her elbow. No one else seemed to notice.

The lift attendant, trained to perfection, fastened his own seat belt, pressed the button marked UP with the index finger of his right hand, and took them up to the third floor. When they had unbuttoned their seat belts and were leaving the lift he saluted again.

Napoleon led them along a corridor and into a huge reception room where a dozen secretaries sat staring into space. There clearly wasn't anything for them to do. Napoleon asked Tom and Dorothy to stay where they were and approached a receptionist at the end of the room. He explained who he'd brought. The receptionist, looking pleased or relieved or possibly both, nodded and spoke.

'Sir Czardas will see you immediately,' Napoleon told Dorothy. 'You must be very important. I've known people wait days even when they had appointments.' He turned to Tom. 'Would you mind coming with me? The appointment only mentions Dorothy Cobleigh.'

'That's fine,' said Tom.

'We'll go and have a drink and watch football,' said Napoleon. 'We have some old film of football matches from the 20th century.'

'Great', said Tom, who hated football. 'That will be nice.'

Chapter 39

'We had quite a job finding you,' said Sir Czardas.

'I wasn't hiding,' said Dorothy.

'No, no, not at all. Obviously not,' said Sir Czardas. 'It's just that our records aren't quite as good as they used to be.'

'Why did you want to find me?' asked Dorothy.

'A very natural question,' said Sir Czardas. 'But if you don't mind I'd like the Chief Commissioner to tell you that herself' He leant forwards a little, as though about to impart a piece of secret information. 'If you have any concerns about the meeting I think I can reassure you. I'm confident that you will be pleasantly surprised by what the Chief Commissioner has to say to you.' He paused and smiled at her. When he smiled he looked like a pantomime villain, Captain Hook in Peter Pan perhaps, leering at his next victim. It wasn't his fault and he didn't mean to look that way. It was just the way he smiled.

He himself took Dorothy down the corridor to the Chief Commissioner's office suite.

It has been a long time since Sir Czardas had treated any suspect so well.

Chapter 40

'You made that?' demanded the Chief Commissioner, pointing towards the bust on her windowsill. She had expected to be disappointed by Dorothy but she wasn't. Not in the slightest. Dorothy was far older than the sort of woman who attracted her personally (she changed her personal assistants every six months to keep them young and fresh) but she looked interesting and intelligent and capable and, given the circumstances, that was all she wanted of her.

'Oh crumbs!' said Dorothy, tempted to giggle. It had been a long time since she'd giggled. The bust was one she'd made when she was a student. She thought it primitive and rather clumsy. She couldn't even remember who had modelled for it. Almost certainly one of her fellow students.

'Did you make that?' demanded the Chief Commissioner again.

'Yes,' said Dorothy, the giggling moment now over. 'Yes, I made that.'

'I like it,' said the Chief Commissioner. 'It's a wonderful piece of art.'

'Thank you,' said Dorothy.

'I like art,' said the Chief Commissioner. She waved a hand around the room. 'As you can see.'

Dorothy followed the hand with her eyes. She was tempted to giggle again, but didn't. She'd never seen such a mish-mash of furniture in one place. She had, she thought, seen more thought put into a display of furniture in an auction room.

'I want you to make me some statues,' said the Chief Commissioner, who wasn't a woman to waste time on small talk. Especially not with suspects. She'd been surprised about Dorothy being a suspect. But it wasn't the end of the world. And certainly not the end of the project.

'Statues?'

'Statues,' repeated the Chief Commissioner. She pointed to the bust. 'Like that one but with chests and bodies and arms and legs.'

'Yes,' agreed Dorothy who knew what a statue was. 'Exactly.'

'Can you action that?'

'Oh yes.'

'I want to celebrate the wonderful work done by EUDCE,' said the Chief Commissioner. 'Our work is not always fully appreciated.'

Dorothy didn't quite know what to say to this. So she asked a question.

'Who would be the subject?'

'The subject?'

'The model for the statue?'

'Oh, it doesn't really matter.'

'Yourself?'

The Chief Commissioner felt herself blushing. 'Myself?'

'A statue of yourself?'

'Well, do you think that would be artistically online?'

'Oh yes,' said Dorothy who didn't particularly like doing it but who could butter with the best. 'You'd make a splendid subject for a statue.'

The Chief Commissioner blushed an even deeper shade of red. 'Well I dare say that would be...' she searched for a word. 'Acceptable,' she said at last. 'I have no doubt it would make my people very happy.'

There was a silence for a moment. Dorothy didn't know what to say and the Chief Commissioner was clearly imagining the statue of herself

'But I don't just want the one.'

'Not just one statue?'

'No. Not just one. Rather more than one.'

'How many were you thinking of?'

'My door's open on that one but let's say just over eight thousand to start with,' said the Chief Commissioner. 'Say eight thousand and one, perhaps?'

Dorothy stared at her and only managed to stop her jaw dropping by clenching her teeth. 'Eight thousand and one statues?'

'That would be the starting point,' said the Chief Commissioner.

'What would you like the statues made of?' asked Dorothy.

'Terracotta,' said the Chief Commissioner immediately.

And then Dorothy, who had, as a student, actually visited the Terracotta army in China, knew and understood. It was quite a shock to realise just how mad a Chief Commissioner could be, and the heights to which her sense of grandeur could aspire.

'The thing is,' continued the Chief Commissioner, 'brown is such an unfetching colour.' She leant forward and lowered her voice, as though the next bit of the sentence included something of great importance. 'They would be a browny sort of colour wouldn't they?'

'They would,' agreed Dorothy. 'That's the sort of general terracotta colour. Brownish red.'

'Could you perhaps paint them EUDCE blue? You don't need to dress them, of course. That would make them look like window display models. Just paint blue uniforms on them. With little yellow stars.'

'Blue? With yellow stars?'

'That would be nice, don't you think? Artistic? A celebration of EUDCE. Creating a work of art to celebrate the glory of the United States of Europe, formerly the European Union, formerly the European Economic Community, formerly the Common Market. That sort of thing. Great artistic achievement. Grand. Magnificent. And sponsored by the world's greatest ever art patron.' She looked at Dorothy and smiled and then added. 'EUDCE,' she added quickly. 'EUDCE being the greatest ever art patron.'

'Absolutely,' agreed Dorothy. She swallowed hard. 'That would be very artistic,' she agreed.

'We'd want more later,' said the Chief Commissioner. She stood up and started to pace around the room, as she did when she felt particularly excited by some great venture. She liked to think of herself as a visionary, a dreamer. 'I want to make a statement. A statement to celebrate our great achievements.'

'Would you like all eight thousand statues to be in your likeness?' asked Dorothy.

The Chief Commissioner looked at her sharply. 'Good heavens, no!' she said. 'This isn't an exercise in vanity. Mix them about a bit. You can do that can't you? Change the faces. The bodies can be the same. Just change the faces.' She thought for a moment. 'We could even have some men in there,' she said, albeit slightly reluctantly. She thought about this for a while. 'We could have some of our great ones,' she said. 'Do a statue of the great Edward Heath. You remember him, don't you?'

'Oh yes,' said Dorothy.

'And the great Lords Mandelson and Kinnock.'

'Right,' said Dorothy.

'Two Kinnocks,' said the Chief Commissioner, remembering. 'There should be two Kinnocks. One male, one female.'

'Of course.'

'I'll need quite a lot of terracotta,' said Dorothy. 'And some help. I'll have to hire a lot of assistants.'

'Of course you will,' said the Chief Commissioner.

'And I'll need somewhere to make the statues.'

'Of course, of course,' agreed the Chief Commissioner. 'See Sir Czardas about all that. He'll fix you up with whatever you need.' She picked up the telephone. 'I'll tell him to get you whatever you want,' she said. She thought for a moment. 'I'll see that you and your family get extra food coupons. And if your work is satisfactory I'll think about making you a sprout.'

'Thank you,' said Dorothy.

The Chief Commissioner turned to the telephone and waved a hand of dismissal.

'Goodbye,' said Dorothy, heading for the door.

But the Chief Commissioner was already busy talking to Sir Czardas and telling him to get Dorothy as much terracotta as she needed.

'Where do I find it?' asked Sir Czardas.

'How the hell should I know?' demanded the Chief Commissioner. 'Just find it.' And she slammed the telephone down. As she did so it occurred to her that she wasn't even sure what terracotta was. But that wasn't her problem. She walked across to the windowsill and stood in front of the bust she so admired. Eight thousand statues. Eight thousand and one. And more to follow. And at least one of them a likeness of her. Maybe she'd been hasty in telling the sculptor not to make them all like her. Maybe she'd have another word with the woman later. And she'd have to think of where to put the statues when they were made. They could fill the old House of Commons with them. And the House of Lords. They were empty buildings and would make a nice setting for a few hundred statues. And maybe they could use a football stadium. No, that would be no good. The statues might be damaged if it rained. Then she remembered that the English, in the dying days of their existence as a race, had built a football stadium with a moveable roof. She could close the roof and put them in there. How many would that hold? Around 100,000 in the stands. They could rip out all the seats. And another 100,000 on the pitch. And there were other stadiums weren't there? She smiled. This was going to be better than anything the Chinese had done. When it was all finished she'd invite the Life-time President of EUDCE over from Brussels. He could do the official opening. She almost purred. Tony might even bless her. One of his personal blessings rather than one of the communal ones. She shivered with excitement. She pressed the intercom on her desk and told her personal assistant to come in.

Chapter 41

'And she has the power to order 8,001 statues all by herself?'

'It seems so,' replied Dorothy. 'I got the impression she runs the region as though she owns it. A sort of personal fiefdom. I don't think the last Queen of England had a zillionth as much power as she has.'

'They're loaded with money and stuff,' said Tom. 'They've got everything in the world in that place. While you were with Her Highness, Napoleon took me into the sprouts' bar and offered me a choice of nine different malt whiskys.'

'You should have seen the furniture in her office,' said Dorothy. 'It was all beautiful furniture. Each piece worthy of a place in a museum. But together it looked like a badly organised shop. Do you remember that antique shop on the King's road which catered for rich Arabs and Russians?'

Tom laughed at the thought. In the olden days, just before the final rise of EUDCE and the final fall of England, they had sometimes walked into the shop, pretending to browse. They'd once watched the owner sell a Russian oligarch a Chippendale desk and a Louis Quinze chair as a 'nice pair'. When the Russian had sat in the chair and commented about how well it went with the desk they'd had to rush out of the shop in giggles. They'd laughed a lot more in those days.

Napoleon and the stout sprout had driven them home. Sitting in the car neither of them had dared talk about what they'd seen or learnt. There was a glass partition between the two of them and the sprouts sitting in the front but neither Tom nor Dorothy were naive enough to imagine that the back of the car, where they were sitting in comfort, would not be bugged. They had collected Tom's aunt from Gladwys and Dalby's flat (they had insisted that Napoleon take her and Tabatha there before they'd agreed to accompany him to the EUDCE Headquarters) and were back in their kitchen.

'She wants to outdo the Chinese Terracotta Army?'

'Yes.'

'So, presumably she wants the statues to be bigger.'

'She wants more of them.'

'Yes. But she also wants them bigger?'

'I suppose so. She certainly wouldn't say no if they were bigger.'

'Say, seven foot tall?'

'That would be OK. As long as it was measured in metres!'

'The Chinese soldiers are hollow aren't they?'

'The legs are solid, so that they are strong enough to hold up the weight of the bodies. But, yes, the bodies are hollow. The heads, arms and bodies are hollow.'

'Yours will be hollow too?'

'Yes. Otherwise they'd weigh too much. And they'd use up a lot more terracotta.'

'You'd make them in two halves and then glue them together?'

'Yes.'

'The sprouts won't know how much a terracotta statue should weigh?'

'I don't so I don't expect they will. I doubt if anyone has ever weighed one.'

'You could put something into the hollow of the body?'

'Yes, I suppose you could,' agreed Dorothy. 'What sort of something?'

'If you had something solid inside the statues you wouldn't need to have solid legs?'

Dorothy thought for a moment. 'No, I don't suppose so.'

Tom sat back and grinned.

'What on earth are you planning?' asked Dorothy.

'We could hide things inside the terracotta statues,' said Tom.

'Yes, I gathered that!' said Dorothy. 'But what?'

'Think about it,' said Tom. Dorothy thought about it. And thought about it.

And then she knew.

'Oh my God!' she said suddenly.

Chapter 42

Dorothy was given the use of a disused Tesco supermarket in the centre of the town where she and Tom lived. Supermarkets had died a relatively fast death as the oil price had soared. The cost of moving food and other goods around the world (and, indeed, around the country) had risen so far and so fast that the increase in transport costs had put the supermarkets out of business. The little shops that replaced them sold locally grown produce and locally made clothing. Most small shops sold a bit of everything because instead of offering specialist services they catered for the needs of local communities.

'We'll need a constant supply of the coarse, porous clay we need,' Dorothy told the sprout, a seconded Senior Administrative Officer (Shredding) who had been given the specific task of making sure that Dorothy's commission to produce 8,001 statues was not hindered by a lack of resources.

'I can have it delivered to the goods yard at the railway station,' said the sprout. 'But I don't know how we're going to move it from there to Tesco's.'

'Do you mind if we refer to the place where I'll be working as the studio?' asked Dorothy. 'I don't like to think of myself as working in Tesco's.'

The sprout, well aware that the project had been initiated by the Chief Commissioner, offered no objection.

'If you can give me authority to hire some suspects, and a little money to pay for them to buy bicycles and construct trailers I can get the clay moved,' said Dorothy.

The sprout said he thought it unlikely that such permission would be forthcoming. Dorothy said that in that case she'd be quite happy to forget about the 8,001 statues and would the sprout be kind enough to let the Chief Commissioner know that the project had been cancelled for lack of a few bits of scrap wood and some bicycles. The sprout, rather pale, hurried off to his boss, who on hearing that the project had been authorised by the Chief Commissioner herself, called Dorothy into her office.

'There are rules about this sort of thing,' said the sprout, standing up and pointing to a chair. Dorothy sat down. The sprout sat down.

'First you must work out what you need, then you triple it, then you double that and ask for twice as much,' she said. 'We won't give you that, of course. You'll be lucky if you get half. But we will be impressed by the numbers – no one here will take you seriously if you say you can do whatever it is you're doing cheaply – and well pleased that we've been able to cut you down. You'll get far more than you need and I'll get brownie points because I've cut the costs.'

Dorothy did some sums in her head and quoted a final figure.

'Fine,' said the sprout. She wrote down the figure Dorothy had given her on a large form and pushed the form across the desk. 'Sign here, please.' Dorothy signed the form and the sprout picked it up. 'Would you wait here, please?' She stood. 'I'll need to go and arrange for your application to be approved.' She hurried off. 'Make yourself at home,' she said, over her shoulder.

Dorothy leant back and prepared for a long wait. In her experience applications usually took months. She wished she'd smuggled a book in with her. She looked around the office. It was the emptiest office she'd ever seen.

The sprout returned a minute and a half later with approval for all of Dorothy's requirements.

Sir Czardas had taken it upon himself not to interrupt the Chief Commissioner, who was busy overseeing the arrival, and hanging in her office and along the corridor leading to it, of a collection of Old Masters liberated from the Tate Gallery.

'There's no point in leaving them there,' the Chief Commissioner had explained to her personal assistant. 'No one goes to art galleries and museums. Such a waste for them not to be seen.' Her personal assistant had agreed and praised her public spirit in liberating the paintings so that they could be enjoyed by a discerning, if undoubtedly limited, number of art lovers.

'Give Mrs Cobleigh anything she wants,' said Sir Czardas. 'And give it to her yesterday.'

'You must be very important,' said the sprout to Dorothy. 'I've never known anything like this before.'

Chapter 43

'We're going to have to do something to the bodies,' Tom said. 'We can't just put bodies into the terracotta moulds.'

'I thought they'd go nice and stiff,' said Dorothy. 'Rigor mortis.'

'They'll stay stiff for about a day or two. But they'll start to decompose after three days,' said Tom. 'They'll bloat and start to fall apart. And you'll have body fluids staining the terracotta and oozing out of the feet.'

'Ugh.'

'Exactly. We'll need to embalm them otherwise any sprout who comes within a quarter of a mile of your studio will smell a rat. Or rather more than a rat if you see what I mean.'

'I see what you mean. This is going to be more difficult than I thought. How do we embalm them?'

'I talked to Stan. His Dad used to run a funeral parlour. He still prepares bodies for burial. He'll help us. You bend and flex the muscles to get rid of the rigor mortis and then you inject embalming chemicals into the blood vessels, and you replace the stuff in the body cavities with more embalming chemicals.'

'How long does it take?'

'When a funeral guy does it to prepare a body so that it looks good for the relatives it takes hours but we just want the body to be preserved so that it doesn't start bloating and rotting and stinking.'

'Lovely.'

'No, really. It won't take long.'

'And where do we get the embalming stuff from? I can hardly ask Sir Czardas to get me a tanker full of embalming fluid. He's not the brightest guy in the world but even he is going to wonder why I need embalming fluid to make terracotta statues.'

'It's sorted. Stan says he still has a supplier. He can get all we need.

We can put what we like on the invoice we give to the sprouts.'

'Enough for 8,001 bodies?'

'Sure.'

'Goody.'

Chapter 44

Banging sprouts on the head with a frying pan, as they wandered round your home, was retail killing. But killing 8,001 sprouts was wholesale killing.

Instead of killing in kitchens and hallways Tom's small revolutionary army started killing in corridors and stairwells. They killed sprouts as they were about to enter people's homes and they killed them as they were just leaving. And the suspects involved showed great imagination in their use of weapons. A former car mechanic used a tyre lever, a former entertainer used a juggler's Indian club, and a retired serviceman who had been injured in one of Blair's Wars used his spare artificial leg to great effect. But it was the recruitment of a former ten-pin bowling alley proprietor which helped most. He produced a large stash of unwanted skittles which turned out to be perfect, in both weight and size, for killing sprouts. The uniformity of the weapons made it easier for new suspects to be trained, and evening classes were organised where tyro-killers could practise their whirling and smashing. (Until they destroyed them all they used a collection of dress shop mannequins as practice targets.)

Tom's army killed income tax inspectors, value added tax inspectors, health and safety officers and planning officers. They killed sprouts who marched into homes demanding to measure windows, search for labels or inspect the Telescreen. They killed officious bureaucrats who clutched books of rules like rednecked Christian fundamentalists clutch bibles. They killed anyone working for EUDCE. And they discovered that killing, like crochet and most other things, becomes easier the more you do it. They were equal opportunity killers. They killed Christian sprouts, Muslim sprouts, Jewish sprouts, Buddhist sprouts, Episcopalian sprouts, Atheist sprouts and Agnostic sprouts. They killed fat, female sprouts; thin, male sprouts; fat, male sprouts and thin, female sprouts. They killed with due regard for the legislation demanding equality for all. They were multicultural killers. They killed white sprouts, brown sprouts, black sprouts and grey sprouts. No one wearing the uniform of a sprout was spared solely because of his colour, race, creed or ethnicity. In that, if that alone, the killing abided by the laws of

EUDCE.
Gentle, quiet, sensitive people who would have thought twice about killing a mouse found themselves carving notches on their skittles.

Chapter 45

The killing was surprisingly easy to organise.

The sprouts, full of conceit and self-satisfaction, were, on the whole, still unsuspicious. It wasn't too difficult to catch them unawares. And finding assassins wasn't difficult either. Tom put Dalby and Gladwys in charge of recruiting killers while he supervised the purchase of bicycles and the building of trailers for transporting terracotta. Naturally, having the bicycles and the trailers made it easy to move the bodies around.

Dalby and Gladwys stuck to recruiting people over fifty for several reasons.

First, only the older suspects seemed in the slightest bit interested in doing anything to improve their lives. It was only the older suspects who remembered life as it had been in days before the creation of the European Superstate and who realised, therefore, that it was perfectly possible to live in a world where there was more freedom and fewer rules than the world created by EUDCE.

Second, only the older suspects were strong enough, and quick-witted enough, to spot an opportunity (and to take advantage of the opportunity) to down a sprout with a single blow. And only older suspects had the presence of mind to work out what to do with the body afterwards. Younger suspects, who had never faced any real challenges, who had been fast-tracked through the final days of a deteriorating and now non-existent educational system which existed to meet political targets (and therefore ensure that politicians and teachers all received their bonuses), and who had been brought up to believe everything they heard and saw on the Telescreen, were virtually incapable of original thought.

'Most of today's kids seem to think they're entitled to a life full of answers without ever having to wake themselves up long enough to wonder what the questions might be, let alone to ask them,' said Dalby. 'They all have expectations which would embarrass royal princes.'

The one big problem they had lay in moving the sprouts from the places where they'd been turned into bodies, to the place where they would be embalmed and fitted inside their terracotta suits. This was potentially the most dangerous part of the whole exercise, even though Tom's fleet of bicycles and trailers made it practicable. There was always the risk that a sprout would inspect a trailer and find a body. It would be difficult to explain.

Strangely, it was Tom's aunt who (more by accident than design, it is true) made it possible for them to move bodies around without fear of being stopped by the sprouts.

She was towing a trailer full of fresh clay to the studio when she was stopped and arrested by two sprouts who knew nothing about the project. They took her to a local police station. Several hours after her disappearance, a frantic Tom eventually found her. He spoke to Dorothy who immediately insisted on being allowed to telephone Sir Czardas.

'The whole project is abandoned,' she said. 'We're all walking out and going home.'

'Wait, wait, wait!' cried Sir Czardas, terrified and already imagining his new future checking out faded labels on grey underwear. 'What's the problem?'

'The police have arrested one of our cyclists,' said Dorothy, who didn't have to fake her fury. 'How can I possibly move clay to my studio if the police are going to interfere all the time?'

Sir Czardas was almost comically apologetic. He promised to have the two policemen transferred to sentry box duty outside the Scottish Regional Parliament. He promised to have them transported to Africa. He promised to have them handed over to the Americans so that they could be hung, shot or electrocuted or all three. 'I'm having a bad day,' he said. 'Please don't make it any worse. My seventh wife is giving me a hard time because there are three Lady Czardas Tsastskes in existence and the latest one met one of the previous ones while shopping and she wants me to do something about it. What can I do? Moreover, she's constantly worrying about who to invite to her 21st birthday party. I'm on my seventh marriage, and sometimes I wonder if the problem might be me. But in my position I can't afford self-doubts. Do you think there's any chance whatsoever that we can sort this out without you walking away from the project?'

'I just want to be able to have my clay delivered without interference,' said Dorothy, calmer now. She had almost (but most definitely not quite) laughed during Sir Czardas's pitiful revelations.

'That's no problem,' insisted Sir Czardas. He promised that he would give orders that none of Dorothy's bicyclists, or their trailers, would be disrupted by the police. The bicyclists would, he said, be given special passes entitling them to cycle through police cordons, barriers, barricades and, if appropriate, rings of fire.

Dorothy said she thought this would be OK as long as Sir Czardas got the passes sent round within the hour.

The passes were on Dorothy's desk within forty five minutes.

And after that the bicyclists were able to move bodies around just as easily as they were able to move clay around, which is to say that they were able to move it around without any interference whatsoever. Indeed, several of the bicyclists reported that they had been saluted by sprouts, much in the way, said Tom, that motorists had been saluted by RAC and AA patrols back in the 1950's.

Chapter 46

'There is a small problem,' said Sir Czardas. He felt nervous even bringing it up.

'What's that?' demanded the Chief Commissioner. 'We've sorted out our bonuses for the year haven't we?'

'We have,' agreed Sir Czardas.

'And approved them?'

'We did that too.'

'So what else can there be?' she demanded. Her most recent personal assistant had just retired and the Chief Commissioner was impatient. She had a trio of possible replacements waiting outside to be interviewed. Two of them looked particularly attractive. Boyish but elfin. She wondered if she might perhaps just hire them both. It would be easier than making a decision. Then if one turned out to be more acceptable she could keep that one and get rid of the other.

'We seem to have misplaced a number of sprouts recently,' said Sir Czardas.

'Oh, not that nonsense again,' said the Chief Commissioner dismissively. 'You've got a real bee in your bonnet about this,' she added, forgetting that she had originally been the one to bring the matter up.

'I'm sorry, ma'am,' said Sir Czardas. 'But I thought I ought to mention it. Another three hundred went missing last week. I've been told that there are rumours.'

The Chief Commissioner looked up. 'What sort of rumours?' she demanded. She didn't like rumours that she hadn't initiated or didn't control.

'Some of the recruiters tell me that they're having difficulty hiring new replacement sprouts in Poland.'

The Chief Commissioner stared in disbelief.

'I know it sounds unlikely,' agreed Sir Czardas, who had grown to believe that anyone with half a brain would give what cerebral tissue they had left to become a sprout. 'But that's what I'm hearing.' He hesitated. 'I'm told that they seem afraid that they too might disappear,' he added.

'Oh what absolute rubbish!' said the Chief Commissioner who hated inconvenient or unpleasant truths and simply could not believe that EUDCE employees could be frightened of anything. Fear was something EUDCE used as a weapon; it wasn't something they had to deal with themselves. 'I can't bear this sort of nonsense. We have far more important things to worry about.'

'Yes, Chief Commissioner,' agreed Sir Czardas who had not survived in his present position without knowing when to say 'yes' and when to say 'no'.

'And I don't want this sort of rumour spreading!'

'No, Chief Commissioner.'

'Ring up the boss of the BBC and tell him that on no account is any of this nonsense to be broadcast on the Telescreen. If sprouts hear any of this they will be dispirited and disillusioned. If suspects hear it they'll lose all faith in our invulnerability. And if the people in Brussels hear this sort of thing they'll be very upset,' said the Chief Commissioner. She paused and looked at Sir Czardas as though she were looking at him over reading spectacles. 'And quite disapproving.'

'Yes, Chief Commissioner.'

'Do you hear what I'm saying? Do you understand?'

'Yes, Chief Commissioner,' said Sir Czardas, who did on both counts.

'We'll just import more replacement sprouts from Turkey. There are plenty over there who'll jump at the chance to better themselves. We'll give them a signing on bonus. I'll ring someone in Brussels.'

Sir Czardas nodded his understanding, acceptance and approval.

The Chief Commissioner waved a hand dismissively. 'You can go now.'

'Thank you.'

'Send in the first of the three girls waiting outside.'

Chapter 47

The Chief Commissioner was playing the harp. Or, rather, she was attempting to play it. In truth, she couldn't read music and couldn't play the harp. But she had decided that her image would benefit from a little mild eccentricity. So, she had confiscated a harp from a former member of a major orchestra and then hired the harpist as her tutor. Every morning, between 11 a.m. and 11.30 a.m. she had harp lessons. The rest of the time the harp stood in the corner of her office, a constant reminder to everyone who entered that the office's occupant had character. Occasionally, the Chief Commissioner would sit at her harp and pretend that a visitor had interrupted an impromptu recital. This allowed her to pose as an artiste, and enabled her to make her visitor aware that she (or he) was interrupting something important.

'When I came in this morning there were only two guards at the front door,' said the Chief Commissioner. 'There should be four.'

'There should,' agreed Sir Czardas. 'But unfortunately, our personpower situation is a little stretched at the moment. According to the latest report I've had there are another four hundred sprouts missing this week.' He paused, looking for a way to soften the news. 'Taken unofficial leave, I expect,' he added, hoping to ingratiate himself by offering what he suspected would be the Chief Commissioner's own response.

The Chief Commissioner looked at him suspiciously. 'Are you being funny?'

'No, no, not at all,' said Sir Czardas very quickly.

'Good, good,' said the Chief Commissioner. She stared at the ceiling, plucked a couple of harp strings and looked thoughtful. 'And if there is any unhappiness, dissatisfaction, call it what you will, then our new planned celebration will dispel that, don't you think?'

'Celebration?' asked Sir Czardas, nervously wondering if he'd missed something.

'The statues!' said the Chief Commissioner. 'The statues, you nincompoop!'

'Oh yes, of course,' said Sir Czardas. 'The statues will definitely give everyone a real lift.' He paused. 'The thing is,' he said, apologetically, 'we are running rather short of low-level sprouts. And you did say...'

'Oh yes, I was going to ring Brussels about it,' remembered the

Chief Commissioner. 'I'll do it now.' She got up from the harp, moved across to her desk, picked up the telephone and pressed a button. She asked to be connected to one of the permanent members of the Secretariat, a very senior figure in Brussels.

'Mr Deputy President?' said the Chief Commissioner. 'Chief Commissioner Stein, Provincial Commissioner for Administration and Protector of the People for Province 17.' She listened for a moment. 'Yes, that's the one,' she said. 'Formerly Scotland, Wales, Northern Ireland and England.' She laughed lightly at something the Deputy President had said, and listened again. 'Stein,' she repeated. 'Phyllis.' She listened again. 'Yes, that's right my Lord,' she said. She blushed, paused, listened, blushed lightly and simpered. 'That's marvellous of you to remember.' She listened and simpered again. 'Oh may I? Thank you.' She hesitated. 'Thank you my Lord...Gordon,' she said. 'Are you well... Gordon? Splendid. That's wonderful. It's so nice to touch base with you again. I'm afraid we have a little problem here. We're running a little light on sprouts. Could you...'

She listened for a moment as Lord Gordon spoke.

'That would be marvellous,' she said. 'Turks would be perfect, Gordon. A thousand would be lovely.'

She listened again and put her hand over the mouthpiece. 'Gordon is going to action that and send us a thousand Turks,' she whispered. Sir Czardas, tried to look more delighted than he felt. 'And two hundred mixed Latvians, Croatians and Estonians,' she added, still listening and still whispering. 'He can't promise but he says that some of them may even speak a little English.' It immediately occurred to Sir Czardas that their talents in this direction would probably be limited to 'Give me money. I have a baby to support' or 'This is a hold-up. I have a gun. Give me money or I kill you.' He did not allow this politically incorrect thought to expose itself to the world.

When Lord Gordon had finished speaking the Chief Commissioner spoke again. 'Before you go, Gordon,' she said, 'there is one thing I thought I might mention in the interests of forward planning.' She paused, listened and laughed politely. 'Of course,' she said. 'The thing is, that here in my little neck of the woods we've hit upon a rather wonderful way to boost morale and to encourage the people to recognise the wonderful work done by EUDCE.' She paused and listened again. 'Thank you, Gordon,' she said. 'We're creating a permanent exhibition of statuary as a celebration of EUDCE's magnificent era of leadership, peace and prosperity.' She paused. 'I thought I'd put you on the radar for this one.'

She listened, struggling to hide her irritation and frustration, as Gordon said something.

'Statuary,' she explained, as though talking to a rather dim child with a slight hearing problem. 'Statues. You know, like that one we used to have here in Trafalgar Square. On top of that very tall plinth.'

She listened again and seemed alarmed.

'No, no, no, no, of course not. This is absolutely nothing to do with Nelson,' she said firmly. 'Good heavens no, Gordon. We don't even mention his name unless we have to. No, the whole idea for what we're doing was inspired by the Chinese and their terracotta army.'

Lord Gordon said something.

'The Chinese terracotta army,' repeated the Chief Commissioner. 'The Chinese built a huge army of terracotta statues as a permanent celebration.'

She listened.

'No, you wouldn't have heard anything about it on the news,' she said. 'It all happened a while ago. But the statues are still there. They're underground. A farmer found them.'

Lord Gordon spoke.

'No, I don't know what the farmer was doing underground. Maybe he fell down a hole. Or was digging deep trenches or something. Anyway he found all these terracotta soldiers. They were on the Telescreen.'

She listened.

'Terracotta,' she said. 'It's a sort of brown pottery. Made out of some sort of clay.'

Lord Gordon said something.

'Yes, like flower pots,' she said. She looked at Sir Czardas and raised an eyebrow in disbelief. 'Yes, like flower pots.'

She listened.

'No, no, they're much bigger than flower pots. Each statue is about two metres tall.'

Lord Gordon asked something.

'Eight thousand and one of them to start with,' said the Chief Commissioner. 'But we're going to have more. Far more. I want it to be far bigger than anything the Chinese ever imagined.' A thought occurred to her. 'Maybe we should invite some Chinese people over for the grand unveiling. We have a sculptor making the models. Very talented, very well-known sculptor. She's got a lot of assistants, of course.'

She listened.

'Oh yes, the people love it. They adore it. They think it's an absolutely marvellous idea. It's really going to bring us all together in our shared respect for EUDCE.'

She listened as Lord Gordon spoke.

'It was my idea,' she replied and then listened. 'Thank you, very much, Gordon. You're very kind.' She listened again. This time Lord Gordon spoke for several minutes.

'Yes, I think we could do that,' said the Chief Commissioner, clearly surprised but delighted. She covered the telephone mouthpiece and whispered to Sir Czardas. 'Gordon wants to know if we can send our sculptor over there to set up a similar sort of operation for the other regions. We can do that can't we?'

Sir Czardas nodded firmly.

'I'll arrange it today,' said the Chief Commissioner firmly. 'Thank you, Gordon. Thank you very much.' And, after waiting to make sure that Gordon had gone, she put down her telephone.

'Gordon is very excited about the statues project,' she announced. 'He says it's the sort of 360 degree thinking he likes. He thinks it will be just the thing EUDCE needs to make everyone realise just what a wonderful job we've all been doing. He's very, very enthusiastic and very much wants to come to the party. He's rushed off to organise a Report and a Meeting so that they can decide where to put all their statues. His first thought was that to start with they could use those European Parliament buildings. They're hardly ever used now.'

'Marvellous,' said Sir Czardas. 'Very satisfactory.' He paused. 'And he's sending us some sprouts?'

'Definitely,' said the Chief Commissioner. 'Absolutely.' She beamed. 'Would you like some afternoon tea?' she asked. 'My new girl makes absolutely marvellous little sandwiches. Much better than the ones that last one used to make. She only uses the very straightest cucumbers.'

Chapter 48

Tom, Dorothy and Tom's aunt were in their kitchen eating soup that Dorothy had made, using three potatoes, a carrot and a leek that Tom had brought home from the allotment. Despite all the work they were doing on the statues Tom hadn't given up his job. He liked the feeling of security it gave him. Who knew when the statue project might come to an end?

When there was a knock on the front door Tom looked up at Dorothy and shook his head. 'Leave it,' he said.

'It might be a chap about some clay I've ordered,' said Dorothy. 'I told him to call round and let me know as soon they'd heard when the delivery would come in.'

Reluctantly Tom opened the door.

'Difficult to find you at home,' said a sprout in a blue suit.

'Out a lot aren't you?' said the other.

'We're Residential Placement Officers,' said the first sprout. He smirked, knowing the effect this would have.

'Aren't you going to invite us in?' asked the second sprout. 'Not that we need an invitation,' said the first, brushing past Tom and moving into their narrow hallway. He looked around. 'Lots of space,' he said. He opened the door to the living room. 'Very spacious. How many of you are there living here?'

'Three,' replied Tom. 'Myself, my wife and my aunt.'

'Who is it?' called Dorothy.

'It's two Residential Placement Officers,' answered Tom. There was a pause.

'I could do with your help,' Tom called to his wife. 'To show them round.'

'I'll be right there,' answered Dorothy. 'I'll just wash the saucepan.'

'I'll get the frying pan!' cried Tom's aunt. She sounded very excited.

'The two ladies are cooking,' explained Tom. 'Would you like to see upstairs? Shall I lead the way?'

'There's no gate at the top of the stairs,' said the first sprout, looking upwards. He took out a small notebook. 'Have to report that,' he said. He made a note about the missing gate. Tom made a mental note to burn the notebook afterwards.

'Somebody could easily fall down without a gate at the top of the stairs,' said the second sprout.

'Yes,' replied Tom. He tried to sound surprised and grateful. 'I suppose they could. I hadn't thought of that.' He looked again at the two men. The fat one was actually very fat. He was going to be a bugger to get into the trailer. And they might have to put him inside one of the extra large sized statues. 'I'll follow you both up,' he said. 'My wife will be with us in a moment.'

The Beginning of the End

If you enjoyed this book we would be grateful if you would post a review on Amazon.

Vernon Coleman is the author of over 100 books, many of which are now available as kindle books on Amazon. For a full booklist please see the Vernon Coleman page on Amazon.

Printed in Great Britain
by Amazon